Romance

A few moments later she *felt* without seeing when Varo came to stand directly at her shoulder. He was greeted warmly by everyone, but it was Ava he had come for.

"I hope you realise, Ava, as I am the captain of the winning team you owe me a dance. Several, in fact," he said, with his captivating smile.

"Of course, Varo."

She turned to him, her eyes ablaze in her face, brilliant as jewels. Inside she might feel pale with shock, but outside she was all colour—the golden mane of her hair, dazzling eyes, softly blushed cheeks, lovely deep pink mouth. She was determined now to play her part, her only wish to get through the night with grace.

For all he hadn't been completely honest with her, Juan-Varo de Montalvo would never leave her memory—even when he disappeared to the other side of the world.

ARGENTINIAN IN THE OUTBACK

BY
MARGARET WAY

First published in Great Britain 2012
by Mills & Boon, an imprint of Harlequin (UK) Limited.
Harlequin (UK) Limited, Eton House, 18-24 Paradise Road,
Richmond, Surrey TW9 1SR

© Margaret Way, Pty., Ltd 2012

ISBN: 978 0 263 22757 4

Harlequin (UK) policy is to use papers that are natural, renewable and recyclable products and made from wood grown in sustainable forests. The logging and manufacturing process conform to the legal environmental regulations of the country of origin.

Printed and bound in Great Britain
by CPI Antony Rowe, Chippenham, Wiltshire

Margaret Way, a definite Leo, was born and raised in the subtropical River City of Brisbane, capital of the Sunshine State of Queensland, Australia. A Conservatorium-trained pianist, teacher, accompanist and vocal coach, she found her musical career came to an unexpected end when she took up writing— initially as a fun thing to do. She currently lives in a harbourside apartment at beautiful Raby Bay, a thirty-minute drive from the state capital, where she loves dining *al fresco* on her plant-filled balcony, overlooking a translucent green marina filled with all manner of pleasure craft: from motor cruisers costing millions of dollars, and big, graceful yachts with carved masts standing tall against the cloudless blue sky, to little bay runabouts. No one and nothing is in a mad rush, and she finds the laid-back village atmosphere very conducive to her writing. With well over one hundred books to her credit, she still believes her best is yet to come.

Books by Margaret Way:

THE CATTLE KING'S BRIDE
MASTER OF THE OUTBACK
IN THE AUSTRALIAN BILLIONAIRE'S ARMS
HER OUTBACK COMMANDER
AUSTRALIA'S MAVERICK MILLIONAIRE

**These books are also available in eBook format
from www.millsandboon.co.uk**

CHAPTER ONE

THE French doors of her bedroom were open to the cooling breeze, so Ava was able to witness the exact moment the station Jeep bearing their Argentine guest swept through the tall wrought-iron gates that guarded the main compound. The tyres of the vehicle threw up sprays of loose gravel, the noise scattering the brilliantly coloured parrots and lorikeets that were feeding on the beautiful Orange Flame Grevilleas and the prolific White Plumed species with their masses of creamy white perfumed flowers nearby.

As she watched from the shelter of a filmy curtain the Jeep made a broad half-circle around the playing fountain before coming to a halt at the foot of the short flight of stone steps that led to Kooraki's homestead.

Juan-Varo de Montalvo had arrived.

She didn't know why, but she felt *excited*. What else but excitement was causing that flutter in her throat? It had been a long time since she had felt like that. But why had these emotions come bubbling up out of nowhere? They weren't exactly what one could call appropriate. She had nothing to get excited about. Nothing at all.

Abruptly sobered, she turned back into the room to check her appearance in the pierglass mirror. She had dressed simply: a cream silk shirt tucked into cigarette-slim beige trousers. Around her waist she had slung a wide tan leather belt that showed off her narrow waist. She had debated what to do with her hair in the heat, but at the last moment had left it long and loose, waving over her shoulders. Her blonde hair was one of her best features.

Cast adrift in the middle of her beautifully furnished bedroom, she found herself making a helpless little gesture indicative of she didn't know what. She had greeted countless visitors to Kooraki over the years. Why go into a spin now? Three successive inward breaths calmed her. She had read the helpful hint somewhere and, in need of it, formed the habit. It *did* work. Time to go downstairs now and greet their honoured guest.

Out in the hallway, lined on both sides with gilt-framed paintings, she walked so quietly towards the head of the staircase she might have been striving to steal a march on their guest. Ava could hear resonant male voices, one a little deeper, darker than the other, with a slight but fascinating accent. So they were already inside the house. She wasn't sure why she did it but, like a child, she took a quick peek— seeing while remaining unseen—over the elegant wrought-iron lace of the balustrade down into the Great Hall.

It was then she saw the man who was to turn her whole life upside down. A moment she was destined never to forget. He was in animated conversation with her brother, Dev, both of them standing directly beneath the central chandelier with all its glittering, singing crystal drops. Their body language was proof they liked and respected each other, if one accepted the theory that the distance one maintained between oneself and another said a great deal about their relationship. To Ava's mind these two were *simpatico*.

Both young men were stunningly handsome. Some inches over six feet, both were wide through the shoulders, lean-hipped, with hard-muscled thighs and long, long legs. As might be expected of top-class polo players, both possessed superb physiques. The blond young man was her brother, James Devereaux Langdon, Master of Kooraki following the death of their grandfather Gregory Langdon, cattle king and national icon; the other was his foil, his Argentine friend and wedding guest. Juan-Varo de Montalvo had flown in a scant fifteen or so minutes before, on a charter flight from Longreach, the nearest domestic terminal to the Langdon desert stronghold—a vast cattle station bordered to the west and north-west by the mighty Simpson, the world's third-largest desert.

In colouring, the two were polarised. Dev's thick hair was a gleaming blond, like her own. Both of them had the Langdon family's aquamarine eyes. De Montalvo's hair was as black and glossy as a crow's wing. He had the traditional Hispanic's lustrous dark eyes, and his skin was tanned to a polished deep bronze. He was very much a man of a different land and culture. It showed in his manner, his voice, his gesticulations—the constant movement of his hands and shoulders, even the flick of his head. Just looking down at him caused a stunning surge of heat in her chest that dived low down into her body, pretty much like swallowing a mouthful of neat whisky.

There was far too much excitement in her reaction, even if it was strictly involuntary. She was a woman who had to defend her inner fortress which she had privately named Emotional Limbo. Why not? She was a woman in the throes of acrimonious divorce proceedings with her husband Luke Selwyn who had turned nasty, even threatening.

She had long reached the conclusion that Luke was a born narcissist, with the narcissist's exaggerated sense of his own importance. This unfortunate characteristic had been fostered from birth by his doting mother, who loved him above all else. Monica Selwyn, however, had pulled away from her daughter-in-law. Ava was the woman who had taken her son from her. The pretence that she had been liked had been at times more than Ava could bear.

When she'd told Luke long months ago she was leaving him and filing for divorce he had flown into a terrible rage. She would have feared him, only she had tremendous back-up and support from just being a Langdon. Luke was no match for her brother. Why, then, had she married him? She had thought she loved him, however imperfectly. Ava knew she couldn't go on with her life without asking herself fundamental questions.

In retrospect she realised she had been Luke's trophy bride—a Langdon with all that entailed. Her leaving him, and in doing so rejecting him, had caused Luke and his establishment family tremendous loss of face. That was the truth of the matter. *Loss of face.* She hadn't broken Luke's heart, just trampled his colossal pride. But wasn't that a potentially dangerous thing for any woman to do to a vain man?

Luke would mend. She was prepared to bet her fortune on that. Whereas she now had a sad picture of herself as a psychologically damaged woman.

Maybe everyone was damaged—only it came down to a question of degree? Some would say one couldn't *be* damaged unless one allowed it, furthermore *believed* it. Unfortunately she had. She felt she was a coward in some ways: afraid of so many things. Afraid to trust. Afraid to stand her ground. Afraid to reach out. Almost afraid to move on. That hurt. For all her lauded beauty, at her core was painfully low self-esteem. Her skin was too thin. She knew it. Pain could reach her too easily.

Ava had lived most of her life feeling utterly powerless: the *granddaughter*, not the all-important *grandson* of a national icon. In her world it was *sons* who were greatly to be prized. But surely that was history? Women through the ages had been expected to make as good a marriage as possible, to honour and obey her husband and bear him children. In some privileged cases for the continuation of the family dynasty.

She didn't give a darn about dynasty. Yet she had found enough courage—perhaps courage was the wrong word and *defiance* was much better—to fly in the face of her authoritarian grandfather's wishes. He had despised Luke and warned her off him. So had Dev, who'd only had her happiness and wellbeing at heart. She had ignored both of them—to her cost—she had got it badly wrong. Proof of her poor judgement.

It would take her some time before she was able to pick herself up and walk back into mainstream life. She had so many doubts about herself and her strength. Many, many women would understand that. It was a common pattern among besieged women trying so hard to do the right thing, with their efforts totally disregarded or held in contempt by their partners. She sometimes wondered if genuine equality between the sexes would ever happen. Women were still receiving horrific treatment at the hands of men all over the world. Unbearable to think that might remain the status quo.

To be truthful—and she believed she was—she had to own up to the fact she had never been passionate about Luke, or indeed any man. Certainly not the way Amelia was passionate about Dev. That *was* love—once in a lifetime love. In Ava's eyes, one had to be incredibly blessed to find it. Ava was an heiress, but she knew better than anyone that although money could buy just about anything it couldn't buy *love*. Her marriage, she acknowledged with a sense of shame, had been an escape route from her dysfunctional family—most particularly her late grandfather.

Her grandfather's death, however, had brought about swift changes. All for the better. Dev now headed up

Langdon Enterprises, of which Kooraki, one of the nation's leading cattle stations and beef producers, was but an arm; their estranged parents were back together—something that filled her and Dev with joy; and Sarina Norton, Kooraki's housekeeper for many years and her grandfather's not-so-secret mistress, had taken herself off to enjoy *la dolce vita* in Italy, the country of her birth.

And last but not least Sarina's daughter—the long-suffering Amelia—was putting the seal on her life-long unbreakable bond with Dev by getting married to him. Ava had long thought of Dev and Amelia as twin stars, circling a celestial field, never far apart. Now at last they were coming together, after delaying the wedding for some months as a mark of respect for Gregory Langdon's passing.

She now had the honour and privilege of being Amelia's chief bridesmaid—one of three. Together the lives of Dev and Amelia had gained their ultimate purpose. They would have children—beautiful children. Mel was strong. Ava had always been stunned by Mel's strength. Beside Mel she was very conscious of her own frailty. Despite the fact that all her own hopes had vanished like a morning mist she couldn't be happier for them. Dev was gaining a beautiful, clever wife who would be a great asset to the family business enterprises, her parents were gaining a daughter-in-law, and she was gaining the sister she had longed for.

Triumphs all round for the Langdon family. The past had to make way for a bright future. There had to be a meaning, a purpose, a *truth* to life. So far it seemed to Ava she had struggled through her existence. How she longed to take wing! She had suffered through the bad times—surely things could only get better?

From her vantage point it was plain to see their visitor projected the somewhat to be feared "dominant male" aura. Man controlled the world. Man was the rightful inheritor of the earth. In a lucid flash of insight she realised she didn't much like men. Her grandfather had been a terrifying man. But at the end of the day what did all that power and money matter? Both were false idols. Strangely, the dominant-male image didn't bother her in her adored brother. Dev had *heart*. But it put her on her guard against men like Juan-Varo de Montalvo. He looked every inch of his six-three—the quintessential macho male. It surrounded him like a force field. Such men were dangerous to emotionally fragile women wishing to lead a quiet life. In her case, she came with baggage too heavy to handle.

De Montalvo, she had learned from Dev, was the only son and heir of one of the richest land-owners in Argentina—Vicente de Montalvo. His mother was the American heiress Caroline Bradfield, who had eloped with Vicente at the age of eighteen against her parents' violently expressed disapproval. Not that Vicente had been all that much older—twenty-three.

The story had made quite a splash at the time. They must have been passionately in love and remained so, Ava thought with approval and a touch of envy. They were still together. And Dev had told her the bitter family feuding was mercifully long over.

Why wouldn't it be? Who would reject a grandson like Juan-Varo de Montalvo, who made an instant formidable impact. He had the kind of features romance novelists invariably labelled "chiselled". That provoked a faint smile—but, really, what other word could one use? He was wearing a casual outfit, much like Dev. Jeans, blue-and-white open-necked cotton shirt, sleeves rolled up, high polished boots. Yet he still managed to look…the word *patrician* sprang to mind. That high-mettled demeanour was inbred—a certain arrogance handed down through generations of a *hidalgo* family.

Dev had told her the Varo side of the family had its own coat of arms, and de Montalvo's bearing *was* very much that of the prideful Old World aristocrat. His stance was quite different from Dev's New World elegant-but-relaxed posture, Dev's self-assured nonchalance. Only as de Montalvo began moving around the Great Hall with striking suppleness a picture abruptly flashed into her mind. It was of a jaguar on the prowl. Didn't jaguars roam the Argentinian *pampas*? She wasn't exactly sure, but she would check it out. The man was dazzlingly exotic. He spoke perfect English. Why *wouldn't* he speak perfect English? He had an American mother. He would be a highly educated man, a cultured world-traveller.

High time now for her to go downstairs to greet him. She put a welcoming smile on her face. Dev would be expecting it.

The wedding was in a fortnight's time. The bride-to-be, Amelia, was still in Sydney, where she was finishing off work for her merchant bank. Dev was planning on flying there to collect her and their parents and some other Devereaux guests. That meant Ava would be playing hostess to Juan-Varo de Montalvo for a short time.

The season was shaping up to be absolutely brilliant for the great day: the sky was so glorious a blue she often had the fancy she was being drawn up into its density. Despite that, they were all praying the Channel Country wouldn't be hit by one of its spectacular electrical storms that blew up out of nowhere and yet for the most part brought not a drop of rain. For once rain wasn't needed after Queensland's Great Flood—a natural disaster that had had a silver lining. After long, long punishing years of drought, the Outback was now in splendid, near unprecedented condition.

Kooraki was a place of extraordinary wild beauty, with every waterhole, creek, billabong and lagoon brimming with life-giving water that brought an influx of waterbirds in their tens of thousands. So the station was in prime condition—the perfect site for the marriage between her brother and her dear friend Amelia.

Guests were coming from all over the country, and Juan-Varo de Montalvo was, in fact, the first overseas visitor to arrive. In his honour Dev had arranged a polo match and a post-polo party for the coming weekend. Invitations had gone out, generating huge interest. Most Outback communities, with their love of horses, were polo-mad. De Montalvo would captain one team, Dev the other. The two men had forged their friendship on the polo field. Dev had even visited the de Montalvo *estancia*—a huge ranch that ran Black Angus cattle, located not all that far from the town of Córdoba. So here were two polo-playing cattlemen who had every reason to relate to each other.

How Juan-Varo de Montalvo would relate to *her* was an entirely different matter. As she moved, her heart picked up a beat a second. Sometimes the purely physical got the better of the mind. She consoled herself with that thought.

Both men looked up as Ava began her descent of the curving staircase, one slender hand trailing over the gleaming mahogany banister. Ava, herself, had the oddest sensation she was walking on air. Her blood was racing. She felt in no way comfortable, let alone possessed of her usual poise. How could feelings run so far ahead of the rational mind?

"Ah, here's Ava," Dev announced with brotherly pride.

Dev's eyes were on his sister and not on Juan-Varo de Montalvo, whose dark regard was also fixed on the very fair young woman who was making her way so gracefully to them. He had known in advance she was beautiful. Dev had boasted many times that he had a beautiful sister. But the reality far exceeded his expectations. He was used to beautiful women. He was a man who loved women, having grown up surrounded by them—doting grandmothers, aunts, female cousins. He adored his mother. He had three beautiful sisters—one older, very happily married with a small son, his godchild, and two younger, with legions of admirers—but something about this young woman sent a jolt of electricity shafting through his body.

He could see beneath the grace, the serene air and the poise that she was oddly *vulnerable*. The vulnerability seemed inexplicable in a woman who looked like an angel and had grown up as she had, with every material advantage. Dev had told him about her failed marriage. Maybe she saw it as a humiliation? A fall from grace? Maybe she was guilty of heedlessly breaking a heart—or worse, inflicting deliberate pain? He had been brought up to frown on divorce. He had lived with two people—his mother and father—who had made a wonderful life together and lived side by side in great harmony.

She had to tilt her head to look up at him. There was a curiously *sad* look in her jewel-like eyes, the same dazzling aquamarine as her brother's. She had flawless skin, with the luminescence of a pearl. Few women could claim a face so incandescent.

It was in all probability a symptom of jet lag, but he felt a distinct low-pitched hum in his ears. Her smile, lovely and effortlessly alluring, seemed to conceal secrets. He had a certainty it was she who had ended her marriage. A cruel thing for an angel to do. One would expect such coldness only of a young and imperious goddess, who would only be loved for as long as it suited her.

Ava released a caught breath. "Welcome to Kooraki, Señor de Montalvo," she said with a welcome return of her practised poise. Heat was coming off the Argentine's aura. It was enveloping her. "It's a pleasure to have you here." It was necessary to go through the social graces even when she was *en garde* and taking great pains not to show it.

"Varo, please," he returned, taking her outstretched hand. His grip was gentle enough not to crush her slender fingers, but firm enough not to let her escape. "It's a great pleasure to be here. I thought it impossible you could be as beautiful as Dev has often described, but now I find you are even more so."

She felt the wave of colour rise to her cheeks but quickly recovered, giving him a slightly ironic look, as though judging and rejecting the sincerity of his words. "Please—you mustn't pander to my vanity," she returned lightly. She couldn't remember the last time a man had caused her to flush. She didn't like the enigmatic half-smile playing around his handsome mouth either. The expression in his dark eyes with their fringe of coal-black lashes was fathoms deep. She was angry with herself for even noticing.

"I had no such thought," he responded suavely, somehow establishing his male authority.

"Then, thank you."

There was strength behind his light grip on her. As a conductor for transmitting energy, his touch put her into such a charged state it caused an unprecedented flare of sexual hostility. It was as though he was taking something from her that she didn't want to give.

The warning voice in her head struck up again. *You have to protect yourself from this man, Ava. He could burn down all your defences.*

That she already knew.

"I find myself fascinated with Kooraki," de Montalvo was saying, including Dev in his flashing white smile. "It is much like one's own private kingdom. The Outback setting is quite extraordinary."

"From colonial times every man of ambition and means came to regard his homestead as the equivalent of the Englishman's country manor," Dev told him. "Most of the historic homesteads were built on memories of home—which was in the main the British Isles."

"Whereas our style of architecture was naturally influenced by Spain."

Dev turned his head to his sister. "As I told you, Estancia de Villaflores, Varo's home, is a superb example."

"We have much to be proud of, don't we?" de Montalvo said, with some gravitas.

"Much to be grateful for."

"Indeed we do." Brother and sister spoke as one.

Ava was finding de Montalvo's sonorous voice, with its deep dark register, making her feel weak at the knees. She was susceptible to voices. Voice and physical aura were undeniably sensual. Here was a man's man, who at the same time was very much a *woman's* man.

He was dangerous, all right.

Get ensnared at your peril.

They exchanged a few more pleasant remarks before Dev said, "I'm sure you'd like to be shown your room, Varo. That was a very long trip, getting here. Ava will show you upstairs. I hope you like what we've prepared for you. After lunch we'll take the Jeep for a quick tour of the outbuildings and a look at some of the herd. An overview, if you like. We have roughly half a million acres, so we'll be staying fairly close in for today."

"I'm looking forward to it," de Montalvo returned, with a sincere enthusiasm that made brother and sister feel flattered.

"Your luggage is already in your room, Varo," Ava told him, aware she was struggling with the man's magnetism. "One of the staff will have brought it up by now, taking the back entrance." Although de Montalvo had travelled a very long way indeed, he showed no signs whatever of fatigue or the usual jet lag. In fact he exuded a blazing energy.

"So no one is wasting time?" De Montalvo took a small step nearer Ava. An inch or two above average height, Ava felt strangely doll-like. "Please lead on, Ava," he invited. "I am all attention."

That made Dev laugh. "I have a few things to attend to, Varo," he called as his sister and his guest moved towards the grand staircase. "I'll see you at lunch."

"Hasta luego!" De Montalvo waved an elegant hand.

Ava had imagined that as she ascended the staircase she would marshal her defences. Now, only moments later, those defences were imploding around her. She had the sense that her life had speeded up, entered the fast lane. She had met many high-powered people in her life—none more so than her grandfather, who hadn't possessed a shining aura. Neither did Montalvo. It was dark-sided, too complex. It wasn't any comfort to realise she had been shocked out of her safe haven. Worse yet to think she might be shorn of protection.

How could any man do that in a split second? The impact had been as swift and precise as a bolt of lightning. Maybe it was because she wasn't used to exotic men? Nor the way he looked at her—as if he issued an outright challenge to her womanhood. Man, that great force of nature, totally irresistible if he so chose.

The thought angered her. Perhaps it was borne of her sexual timidity? Luke had early on in their marriage formed the habit of calling her frigid. She now had an acute fear that if she weren't very careful she might rise to de Montalvo's lure. He was no Luke. He was an entirely different species. Yet in some bizarre way he seemed familiar to her. Only he was a stranger—a stranger well aware of his own power.

As he walked beside her, with his tantalising lithe grace, glowing sparks might have been shooting off his powerful lean body. Certainly *something* was making her feel hot beneath her light clothing. She who had been told countless times she always appeared as cool as a lily. That wasn't the case now. She felt almost *wild*, when she'd had no intention let alone any experience of being any such thing. To her extreme consternation her entire body had become a mass of leaping responses. If those responses broke the surface it would be the ultimate humiliation.

His guest suite was in the right wing. It had been made ready by the household staff. Up until their grandfather's death the post of housekeeper had been held by Sarina Norton, Amelia's mother. Sarina had been most handsomely rewarded by Gregory Langdon for "services rendered". No one wanted to go there...

The door lay open. Varo waved a gallant arm, indicating she should enter first. Ava had the unsettling feeling she had to hold on to something. Maybe the back of a chair? The magnetic pull he had on her was so strong. How on earth was she going to cope when Dev flew off to Sydney? She was astonished at how challenging she found the prospect. What woman reared to a life of privilege couldn't handle entertaining a guest? She was a woman who had not only been married but was in the process of divorce—she being the one who had initiated the action. Didn't that qualify her as a woman of the world?

Or perhaps one could interpret it as the action of a woman who didn't hesitate to inflict pain and injury? Perhaps de Montalvo had already decided against her? His family of Spanish origin was probably Roman Catholic, but divorce couldn't be as big a no-no now as it had been in the time of Katherine of Aragon, Henry VIII's deposed, albeit lawfully wedded, wife. Not that taking Katherine's place had done Anne Boleyn much good.

Ava put the tension that was coiling tighter and tighter inside her down to an attack of nerves. It was all so unreal.

The guest room that had been chosen for de Montalvo was a grand room—and not only in terms of space and the high scrolled ceilings that were a feature of Kooraki's homestead. The headboard of the king-sized bed, the bed skirt and the big cushions were in a metallic grey silk, with pristine white bed-coverings and pillows. Above the bed hung a large gold-framed landscape by a renowned English-Australian colonial artist. Mahogany chests to each side of the bed held lamps covered in a parchment silk the same colour as the walls. A nineteenth century English secretary, cabinet and comfortable chair held pride of place in one corner of the room. The rest of the space was taken up by a gilded Louis XVI-style sofa covered in black velvet with a matching ottoman. All in all, a great place to stay, with the added plus of a deep walk-in wardrobe and an *en suite* bathroom.

He said something in Spanish that seemed to make sense to her even though she didn't know the language. Quite obviously he was pleased. She did have passable French. She was better with Italian, and she even had some Japanese—although, she acknowledged ruefully, keeping up with languages made it necessary to speak them every day. She even knew a little Greek from a fairly long stint in Athens the year after leaving university.

De Montalvo turned back from surveying the landscaped garden. "I'll be most happy and comfortable here, Ava," he assured her. "I'm sure this will be a trip never to be forgotten."

She almost burst out that she felt the same. Of course she did not. She meant to keep her feelings to herself. "I'll leave you in peace, then, Varo," she said. "Come downstairs whenever you like. Lunch will be served at one. Dev will be back by then."

"Gracias," he said.

Those brilliant dark eyes were looking at her again. Looking *at* her. *Through* her. She turned slowly for the door, saying over a graceful shoulder, *"Nuestra casa es su casa."*

His laugh was low in his throat. "You make a fine attempt. Your accent is good. I hope to teach you many more Spanish phrases before I leave."

Ava dared to face him. "Excellent," she said, her tone a cool parry.

CHAPTER TWO

THEY set out after breakfast the next day, the horses pick-
ing their way through knee-high grasses with little indigo-
blue wildflowers swimming across the waving green
expanses. Dev had flown to Sydney at first light, leaving
them alone except for the household staff. She would have
de Montalvo's company for a full day and a night and several hours of the following day before Dev, Amelia and co
were due to fly back. So, all in all, around thirty hours for
her to struggle against de Montalvo's powerful sexual aura.

For someone of her age, marital status and background
Ava was beginning to feel as though she had been wander-
ing through life with her eyes closed. Now they were open
and almost frighteningly perceptive. Everyone had the experience of meeting someone in life who raised the hackles
or had an abrasive effect. Their Argentine visitor exerted
a force of quite another order. He had *roped* her, in cattleman's terms—or she had that illusion.

Dinner the previous evening had gone off very well. In
fact it had been a beautiful little welcoming party. They'd
eaten in the informal dining room, which was far more
suitable and intimate than the grand formal dining room
only used for special occasions. She'd had the table set with
fine china, sterling silver flatware, and exquisite Bohemian
crystal glasses taken from one the of numerous cabinets

holding such treasures. From the garden she had picked a spray of exquisite yellow orchids, their blooms no bigger than paper daisies, and arranged them to take central pride of place. Two tall Georgian silver candlesticks had thrown a flattering light, finding their reflection in the crystal glasses.

The menu she'd chosen had been simple but delicious: white asparagus in hollandaise, a fish course, the superb barramundi instead of the usual beef, accompanied by the fine wines Dev had had brought up from the handsomely stocked cellar. Dessert had been a light and lovely passion-fruit trifle. She hadn't gone for overkill.

Both Dev and his guest were great *raconteurs*, very well travelled, very well read, and shared similar interests. Even dreams. She hadn't sat back like a wallflower either. Contrary to her fluttery feelings as she had been dressing—she had gone to a surprising amount of trouble—she had found it remarkably easy to keep her end up, becoming more fluent by the moment. Her own stories had flowed, with Dev's encouragement.

At best Luke had wanted her to sit quietly and look beautiful—his sole requirements of her outside the bedroom. He had never wanted her to shine. De Montalvo, stunning man that he was, with all his eloquent little foreign gestures, had sat back studying her with that sexy half-smile hovering around his handsome mouth. Admiring—or mocking in the manner of a man who was seeing exactly what he had expected to see? A blonde young woman in a long silk-jersey dress the exact colour of her eyes, aquamarine earrings swinging from her ears, glittering in the candlelight.

She was already a little afraid of de Montalvo's half-smile. Yet by the end of the evening she had felt they spoke the same language. It couldn't have been a stranger sensation.

Above them a flight of the budgerigar endemic to Outback Australia zoomed overhead, leaving an impressive trail of emerald and sulphur yellow like a V-shaped bolt of silk. De Montalvo studied the indigenous little birds with great interest. "Amazing how they make that formation," he said, tipping his head back to follow the squadron's approach into the trees on the far side of the chain of billabongs. "It's like an aeronautical display. I know Australia has long been known as the Land of the Parrot. Already I see why. Those beautiful parrots in the gardens—the smaller ones—are lorikeets, flashing colour. And the noisy ones with the pearly-grey backs and the rose-pink heads and underparts—what are they?"

"Galahs." Ava smiled. "It's the aboriginal name for the bird. It's also a name for a silly, dim-witted person. You'll hear it a lot around the stockyards, especially in relation to the jackeroos. Some, although they're very keen, aren't cut out for the life. They're given a trial period, and then, if they can't find a place in the cattle world, they go back home to find alternative work. Even so they regard the experience as the adventure of a lifetime."

"I understand that," he said, straightening his head. "Who wouldn't enjoy such freedom? Such vast open spaces virtually uninhabited by man? Our *gauchos* want only that life. It's a hard life, but the compensations are immense. Kooraki is a world away from my home in Argentina," he mused, studying Ava as though the sight of her gave him great pleasure. "There is that same flatness of the landscape. Quechua Indians named our flatness *pampa*—much like your vast plains. But at home we do not know such extreme isolation at this. There are roads fanning out everywhere from the *estancia*, and the grounds surrounding the house— designed many decades ago and established by one of our finest landscape designers—are more like a huge botanical garden. Here it is pure *wilderness*. Beautiful in the sense of not ever having been conquered by man. The colours are indescribable. Fiery red earth, all those desert ochres mixed in beneath dazzling blue skies. Tell me, is the silvery blue shimmer the mirage that is dancing before our eyes?"

"It is," Ava confirmed. "The mirage brought many an early explorer to his grave. To go in search of an inland sea of prehistory and find only great parallel waves of red sand! It was tragic. They even took little boats like dinghies along."

"So your Kooraki has a certain mysticism to it not only associated with its antiquity?"

"We think so." There was pride in her voice. "It's the oldest continent on earth after all." Ava shifted her long heavy blonde plait off her nape. It was damp from the heat and the exertion of a fantastically liberating gallop with a splendid horseman who had let her win—if only just. "You do know we don't call our cattle stations *ranches*, like Americans? We've kept with the British *station*. Our stations are the biggest in the world. Anna Creek in the Northern Territory spreads over six million acres."

"So we're talking thirty thousand square kilometres plus?" he calculated swiftly.

"Thirty-four thousand, if we're going to be precise. Alexandria Station, also in the Territory, is slightly smaller. Victoria Downs Station used to be *huge*."

He smiled at the comparatives. "The biggest ranches in the U.S. are around the three thousand square kilometres mark, so you're talking ten times that size. Argentine *estancias* are nowhere in that league either. Although earlier in the year a million-acre *estancia* in north-west Argentina was on sale, with enormous potential for agriculture—even eco-power possibilities. Argentina—our beautiful cosmopolitan capital Buenos Aires—was built on *beef*, as Australia's fortunes were built on the sheep's back—isn't that so?" He cast her a long glance.

"I can't argue with that. Langdon Enterprises own both cattle and sheep stations. Two of our sheep stations produce the finest quality merino wool, mainly for the Japanese market. Did Dev tell you that?"

"I believe he did. Dev now has a great many responsibilities following your grandfather's death?"

"He has indeed," she agreed gravely, "but he's up to it. He was born to it."

It was her turn to study the finely chiselled profile de Montalvo presented to her. He wasn't wearing the Outback's ubiquitous akubra, but the startlingly sexy headgear of the Argentine *gaucho*: black, flat-topped, with a broad stiff brim that cast his elegant features into shadow. To be so aware of him sexually was one heck of a thing, but she strove to maintain a serene dignity, at the same time avoiding too many of those brilliant, assessing glances.

"Your father was not in the mould of a cattleman?" he asked gently.

Ava looked away over the shimmering terrain that had miraculously turned into an oasis in the Land of the Spinifex. The wake of the Queensland Great Flood had swept right across the Channel Country and into the very Red Centre of the continent.

"That jumped a generation to Dev. He was groomed from boyhood for the top. There was always great pressure on him, but he could handle it. Handle my grandfather as well. The rest of us weren't so fortunate. My father is much happier now that he has handed over the reins. My grandfather, Gregory Langdon, was a man who could terrify people. He was very hard on all of us. Dad never did go along with or indeed fit into the crown-prince thing, but he was a very dutiful son and pleasing his father was desperately important to him."

"And you?"

Ava tilted her chin an inch or so. "How can I say this? I'm chiefly remembered for defying my grandfather to marry my husband. Neither my grandfather nor Dev approved of him. It soon appeared they were right. You probably know I'm separated from my husband, in the process of getting a divorce?"

Varo turned his handsome head sideways to look at her. Even in the great flood of light her pearly skin was flawless. "I'm sorry." Was he? He only knew he definitely didn't want her to be married.

"Don't be," she responded, more curtly than she'd intended. He would probably think her callous in the extreme.

He glimpsed the flash of anger in her remarkable eyes. Obviously she longed to be free of this husband she surely once had loved. What had gone so badly wrong?

"I too tried very hard to please my grandfather," she offered in a more restrained tone. "I never did succeed— but then my grandfather had the ingrained idea that women are of inferior status."

"Surely not!" He thought how his mother and sisters would react to that idea.

"I'm afraid so. He often said so—and he *meant* it. Women have no real business sense, much less the ability to be effective in the so-called 'real' world. Read for that a *man's* world—although a cattle kingdom *is* a man's world it's so tough. Women are best served by devoting their time to making a good marriage—which translates into landing a good catch. Certainly a good deal of time, effort and money went into me."

"This has led to bitterness?" He had read much about the ruthless autocratic patriarch Gregory Langdon.

Ava judged the sincerity of his question. She was aware he was watching her closely. "Do I seem bitter to you?" She turned her sparkling gaze on him.

"Bitter, no. Unhappy, yes."

"Ah…a clarification?" she mocked.

"You deny it?" He made one of his little gestures. "Your husband is not putting up a fight to keep you?" Such a woman came along once in a lifetime, he thought. For good or bad.

Ava didn't answer. They had turned onto a well-trodden track that led along miles of billabongs, creeks and water-holes that had now become deep lagoons surrounded on all sides by wide sandy beaches. The blaze of sunlight worked magic on the waters, turning them into jewel colours. Some glittered a dark emerald, others an amazing sapphire-blue, taking colour from the cloudless sky, and a few glinted pure silver through the framework of the trees.

"One tends to become unhappy when dealing with a divorce," Ava answered after a while. "My marriage is over. I will not return to it, no matter what. Dev at least has found great happiness." She shifted the conversation from her. "He and Amelia are twin souls. You'll like Amelia. She's very beautiful and very clever. She holds down quite a high-flying job at one of our leading merchant banks. She'll be a great asset to Langdon Enterprises. Mercifully my grand-father didn't pass on his mindset to Dev."

"Dev is a man of today. He will be familiar with very successful women. But what do *you* plan to do with your-self after your divorce comes through?"

She could have cried out with frustration. Instead she spoke with disconcerting coolness. "You are really inter-ested?"

"Of course." His tone easily surpassed hers for hauteur.

She knew she had to answer on the spot. Their eyes were

locked. Neither one of them seemed willing to break contact. They could have been on some collision course. "Well, I don't know as yet, Varo," she said. "I might be unequal to the huge task Dev has taken on, but I want to contribute in any way I can."

"Then of course you will." A pause. "You will marry again."

It wasn't a question but a statement. "That's a given, is it? You see it as my only possible course?" she challenged.

He reached out a long arm and gently touched her delicate shoulder, leaving a searing sense of heat. It was as though his hand had touched her bare skin.

"Permit me to say you are very much on the defensive, Ava. You know perfectly well I do not." The sonorous voice had hardened slightly. "Dev will surely offer you a place on the board of your family company?"

"If I want a place, yes," she acknowledged.

He gave her another long, dark probing look. "So you are not really the businesswoman?"

She shook her head. "I have to admit it, no. But I have a sizeable chunk of equity in Langdon Enterprises. Eventually I will take my place."

"You should. There would be something terribly wrong if you didn't. You want children?"

She answered that question with one of her own. "Do you?"

He gave her his fascinating, enigmatic half-smile. "Marriage first, then children. The correct sequence."

"Used to be," she pointed out with more than a touch of irony. "Times have changed, Varo."

"Not in *my* family," he said, with emphasis. "I do what is expected of me, but I make my own choices."

"You have a certain woman in mind?"

It would be remarkable if he didn't. She had the certainty

this dynamic man had a dozen dazzling women vying for his attention.

"Not at the moment, no," he told her with nonchalance. "I enjoy the company of women. I would never be without women in my life."

"But no one as yet to arouse passion?" She was amazed she had even asked the question, and aware she was moving into dangerous territory.

Her enquiring look appeared to him both innocent and seductive at one and the same time. Did she know it? This wasn't your usual *femme fatale*. There was something about her that made a man want to protect her. Possibly that was a big mistake. One her husband had made?

"I don't think I said that," he countered after a moment. "Who knows? I may have already succumbed to *your* undoubted charms, Ava."

She raised a white hand to wave a winged insect away— or perhaps to dismiss his remark as utterly frivolous. "It would do you no good, Varo. I'm still a married woman. And I suspect you might be something of a legend back in Argentina."

"Perdón—perdonare!" he exclaimed. "Surely you mean as a *polo player*?" He pinned her gaze.

Both of them knew she had meant as a *lover*. "I'm looking forward to seeing you in action at the weekend." She declined to answer, feeling hot colour in her cheeks. "It should be a thrilling match. We're all polo-mad out here."

"As at home. Polo is the most exciting game in the world."

"And possibly the most dangerous," she tacked on. "Dev has taken a few spectacular spills in his time."

He answered with an elegant shrug of one shoulder. "As have I. That is part of it. You are an accomplished rider," he commented, his eyes on her slender body, sitting so straight but easy in the saddle. Such slenderness lent her a deceptive fragility, contradicted by the firmness with which she handled her spirited bright chestnut mare.

"I should be." Ava's smile became strained as memories flooded in. "My grandfather threw me up on a horse when I was just a little kid—around four. I remember my mother was beside herself with fright. She thought I would be hurt. He took no notice of her. Mercifully I took to riding like a duck to water. A saving grace in the eyes of my grandfather. As a woman, all that was expected of me was to look good and produce more heirs for the continuation of the Devereaux-Langdon dynasty. At least I was judged capable of expanding the numbers, if not the fortune. A man does that. I expect in his own way so does Dev. Every man wants a son to succeed him, and a daughter to love and cherish, to make him proud. I suppose you know my grandfather left me a fortune? I don't have to spend one day working if I choose not to."

"Why work at anything when one can spend a lifetime having a good time?" he asked on a satirical note.

"Something like that. Only I *need* to contribute."

"I'm sure you shall. You need time to re-set your course in life. All things are possible if one has a firm belief in oneself. Belief in oneself sets us free."

"It's easier to dream about being free than to accomplish it," she said, watching two blue cranes, the Australian brolgas, getting set to land on the sandy banks of one of the lagoons.

"You thought perhaps marriage would set you free?" he shot back.

"I'm wondering if you want my life story, Varo?" Her eyes sparkled brightly, as if tears weren't all that far away.

"Not if you're in no hurry to tell me," he returned gently, then broke off, his head set in a listening position. "You hear that?"

They reined in their horses. "Yes." Her ears too were registering the sound of pounding hooves.

Her mare began to skip and dance beneath her. In the way of horses, the mare was scenting some kind of danger. De Montalvo quietened his big bay gelding with a few words in Spanish which the gelding appeared to understand, because it ceased its skittering. Both riders were now holding still, their eyes trained on the open savannah that fanned out for miles behind them.

In the next moment they had their answer. Runaway horse and hapless rider, partially obscured by the desert oaks dotted here and there, suddenly burst into full view.

De Montalvo broke the fraught silence. "He's in trouble," he said tersely.

"It's a workhorse." Ava recognised that fact immediately, although she couldn't identify the rider. He was crouched well down over his horse's back, clinging desperately to the flowing black mane. Feet were out of the stirrups; the reins were flailing about uselessly. "It's most likely one of our jackeroos," she told him with anxiety.

"And he's heading right for that belt of trees," De Montalvo's expression was grim. "If he can't pull up he's finished. *Terminado!*" He pulled the big bay's head around as he spoke.

The area that lay dead ahead of the station hand's mad gallop was heavily wooded, dense with clumps of ironwood, flowering whitewoods and coolabahs that stood like sentinels guarding the billabong Ava knew was behind them. The petrified rider was in deep trouble, but hanging on for dear life. He would either be flung off in a tumble of broken bones or stay on the horse's back, only to steer at speed into thick overhanging branches. This surely meant a broken neck.

"Stay here," de Montalvo commanded.

It was an order, but oddly she didn't feel jarred by it. There was too much urgency in the situation.

She sat the mare obediently while de Montalvo urged the powerful bay gelding into a gallop. Nothing Zephyr liked better than to gallop, Ava thought with a sense of relief. Nothing Zephr liked better than to catch and then overtake another horse. That was the thoroughbred in him.

The unfortunate man had long since lost his hat. Now Ava recognised the red hair. It was that Bluey lad—a jackeroo. She couldn't remember his surname. But it was painfully clear he was no horseman. One could only wonder what had spooked his horse. A sand goanna, quite harmless but capable of giving a nervous horse a fright? Goannas liked to pick their mark too, racing alongside horse and rider as though making an attempt to climb the horse's sleek sides. A few cracks of the whip would have settled the matter, frightening the reptile off. But now the young jackeroo was heading full pelt for disaster.

Ava held up a hand to shield her eyes from the blazing sun. Little stick figures thrown up by the mirage had joined the chase, their legs running through the heated air. She felt incredibly apprehensive. Señor de Montalvo was their guest. He was a magnificent rider, but what he was attempting held potential danger for him if he persisted with the wild chase. If he were injured… If he were injured… She found herself praying without moving her dry lips.

Varo had been obliged to come at the other horse from an oblique angle. She watched in some awe as he began to close in on the tearaway station horse that most likely had started life as a wild brumby. Even in a panic the workhorse couldn't match the gelding for speed. Now the two were racing neck and neck. The finish line could only be the wall of trees—which could prove to be as deadly as a concrete jungle.

Ava's breath caught in her throat. She saw Varo lean sideways out of his saddle, one hand gripping his reins and the pommel, the other lunging out and down for the runaway's reins. A contest quickly developed. Ava felt terribly shaken, not knowing what to expect. She found herself gripping her own horse's sides and crying out, "Whoa, boy, whoa!" even though she was far from the action. She could see Varo's powerful gelding abruptly change its long stride. He reined back extremely hard while the gelding's gleaming muscles bunched beneath its rider. Both horses were acting now in a very similar fashion. Only a splendid horseman had taken charge of them, bringing them under tight control.

The mad flight had slowed to a leg-jarring stop. Red dust flew in a circling cloud, earth mixed up with pulped grasses and wildflowers. "Thank God!" Ava breathed. She felt bad enough. Bluey was probably dying of fright. What of Varo? What an introduction to their world!

The headlong flight was over. She had a feeling Bluey wasn't going to hold on to his job. She was sure she had heard of another occasion when Bluey had acted less than sensibly. At least he was all right. That was the important thing. There had been a few tragic stories on Kooraki. None more memorable than the death in a stampede of Mike Norton, Sarina Norton's husband but not, as it was later revealed, Amelia's actual father. Sarina Norton was one beautiful but malevolent woman, loyal to no one outside herself.

Ava headed off towards the two riders who had sought the shade to dismount. Her mare's flying hooves disturbed a group of kangaroos dozing under one of the big river gums. They began to bound along with her.

It was an odd couple she found. Bluey, hardly more than a madcap boy, was shivering and shaking, white as a sheet beneath the orange mantling of freckles on his face. Varo showed no sign whatsoever of the recent drama, except for a slick of sweat across his high cheekbones and the tousling of his thick coal-black hair. Even now she had to blink at the powerful magnetism of his aura.

He came forward as she dismounted, holding the mare's reins. They exchanged a measured, silent look. "All's well that ends well, as the saying goes." He used his expressive voice to droll effect. Far from being angry in any way, he was remarkably cool, as though stopping runaway horses and riders was a lesson he had learned long ago.

Ava was not cool. He was their guest. "What in blue blazes was *that* exhibition all about?" she demanded of the hapless jackeroo. She watched in evident amazement as the jackeroo attempted a grin.

"I reckon I oughta stick to motorbikes."

"I've seen you before, haven't I?" Ava asked with a frown.

"Yes, miss." The jackeroo sketched a wobbly bow. "I'm Bluey. This gentleman here did a great job of saving me life. I'd have broken a leg, for sure."

"You'd have broken a great deal more than that," Varo pointed out, this time making no attempt to hide the note of reproof.

"It was a mongrel goanna." Bluey made a wild gesture with his skinny arms. "About six feet long."

"Nonsense!" Ava shook her head. "It was probably a sand goanna, half that size. You must have alarmed it."

"Well, it rushed me anyway," Bluey mumbled, implying anyone would have reacted the same way. "Sprang up from under a tree. I thought it was a damned log, beggin' your pardon."

"Some log!" It was all Ava could do not to tell Bluey off. "You could have frightened it off with a few flicks of the whip."

"Couldn't think fast enough," Bluey confessed, looking incredibly hot and dirty.

The expression on Juan-Varo de Montalvo's handsome face conveyed what he thought of the jackeroo's explanation. "You're all right to mount your horse again?" he addressed the boy with clipped authority in his voice.

"Poor old Elvis." Bluey shook his copper head. "The black mane, yah know? I thought his heart would burst."

"The black mane?" Varo's expression lightened. He even laughed. "I see."

Ava was finding it difficult to keep her eyes off him. He looked immensely strong and capable, unfazed by near disaster. His polished skin glowed. The lock of hair that had fallen forward onto his tanned forehead gave him a very dashing, rakish look. He wore his hair fairly long, so it curled above the collar of his shirt. She tried not to think how incredibly sexy he was. She needed no such distraction.

As they paused in the shade small birds that had been hidden in the safety of the tall grasses burst into the air, rising only a few feet before the predatory hawks made their lightning dives. Panicked birds were caught up, others managed to plummet back into the thick grass. This was part of nature. As a girl Ava had always called out to the small birds, in an effort to save them from the marauding hawks, but it had been an exercise in futility.

"What were you doing on your own anyway, Bluey? You should have been with the men."

Bluey tensed. "Headin' for the Six Mile," he said evasively. "You're not gunna tell the boss, are you?" he asked, as though they shared a fearful secret.

Varo glanced at Ava, who was clearly upset, her eyes sparkling. He decided to intervene. "Get back on your horse. I assume the red hair justifies the nickname! We'll ride with you to the house. You'll need something for those skinned hands."

"A wash up wouldn't hurt either," Ava managed after a moment. "Think you'll be more alert next time a goanna makes a run for your horse?"

"I'll practise a lot with me whip," Bluey promised, some colour coming back into his blanched cheeks. "I hope I didn't spoil your day?"

"Spoil our day?" Ava's voice rose. "It would have been horrible if anything had happened, Bluey. Thank God Varo was with me. I doubt *I* could have caught you, let alone have the strength to bring the horses under control."

"Sorry, miss," Bluey responded, though he didn't look all that troubled. "I could never learn to ride like *you*." Bluey looked to the man who had saved him from certain injury or worse.

"You can say that again!" Ava responded with sarcasm.

"Thanks a lot, mate." Bluey leaked earnest admiration from every pore.

Varo made a dismissive gesture. "M-a-t-e!" He drew the word out on his tongue.

"Well, that's *one* version of it." Ava had to smile. Did the man have any idea what a fascinating instrument his voice was? "Well, come on, Bluey," she said, giving the jackeroo a sharp look. "Get back up on your horse."

Bluey shook himself to attention. "Dunno who got the bigger fright—me or Elvis." He produced a daft grin.

As they rode back to the homestead Ava couldn't help wondering if Bluey would ever make it as a station hand. His derring-do could prove a danger to others. From fright and alarm he had gone now to questioning his hero about life on the Argentine pampas, confiding that everyone— "I mean everyone!"—would be turning up to see him play polo at the weekend. "You got one helluva lot of strength inside you," Bluey told the South American visitor with great admiration.

"Just as well. It was a titanic struggle," Ava said, resisting the impulse to call Bluey the derogatory *galah*. "Common sense goes a long way. If I find you've used up eight lives...?" She paused significantly.

"Please don't tell the boss, miss," Bluey begged. "One more sin and he'll kick me out."

"And there goes your big adventure." Ava shrugged, thinking admonition might well fall on deaf ears. "It could be later than you think, Bluey. Now, let's get you cleaned up."

CHAPTER THREE

WHEN they arrived back at the homestead, Varo sent the jackeroo off to the first-aid room.

"Let me have a word with this young man." He inclined his head towards Ava.

"You think you can talk some sense into him?" she asked sceptically. "I remember now—he once put Amelia in danger with one of his ill-conceived stunts."

"I think I can make him see sense," he answered with quiet authority. "He knows there's a strong possibility he will be sent home if Dev hears about this."

"Maybe we should tell Dev?" she suggested with utter seriousness. "In rescuing Bluey you put yourself at considerable risk."

"One doesn't think of that at such a time." He dismissed the risk factor, looking deeply into her eyes.

"All right," she consented, trying not to appear flustered. "I'll see to lunch. This afternoon I thought I might show you the hill country. It's not all low-rise on Kooraki. The hills reach a fair height. A good climb, anyway—and there's so much to see. Aboriginal rock paintings. And there really *was* an inland sea—but we're talking pre-history. There are drawings of crocodiles on the rock walls. X-ray depictions of fish. We even have a waterfall of sorts at the moment. It plunges downhill into the rock pool beneath it. Not even a trickle in the Dry, of course."

She knew the rock pool would be a great place for a dip. The waters were fairly deep, and crystal-clear, but Juan-Varo de Montalvo made her feel far too aware of herself as a woman to risk donning a bathing suit.

"We will ride there?" he asked, already filled with fascination for the fabled Outback.

She shook her blonde head. "We'll take the Jeep. I'll even let you drive." She gave him a quick smile which he thought as alluring as any water nymph. "There's no wrong side of the road."

"Gracias, Señora," His black eyes glittered as he acknowledged her marital status.

It was quite a job to keep her expression composed. Infatuation was the last thing she had seen coming.

From the passenger window Ava eyed the Wetlands, home to thousands upon thousands of waterbirds. The vast expanse of water had joined up with the lignum swamps to the extent one didn't know where the lignum swamps ended and the Wetlands started up.

"In times of drought this great expanse of water will dry up," she told Varo, who drove like he did everything else. With absolute skill and confidence. "The parched surface becomes crisscrossed by cracks and the footprints of the wildlife—kangaroos, emus, camels, wild pigs, snakes, or any human walking across the dry ochre sand."

"Camels I *have* to see," he said, giving her a quick sidelong smile.

"You will," she promised. "The Afghan traders brought them in the early days. 1840, to be precise. They thrived here. We even export them to Arab countries. They're part of the landscape now, but they can be very destructive. Not as much as hoofed animals, however. Their feet are adapted for deserts. They have soft pads, but they eat everything in sight, depleting the food supply for our indigenous species. They're very dangerous too, when the male goes on heat."

"The *male?*" One black eyebrow shot up.

"Bizarre, but true. At the last count there were over a million feral camels scattered over the desert areas of the Territory, Western Australian, South Australia and Queensland's desert fringe. The introduced water buffalo of the Territory do tremendous damage to the environment and the ecosystem. Even our dingoes were introduced."

"But I thought they were native Australian animals?" He glanced back at her. She had taken her beautiful hair out of its plait. Now it was sliding over her shoulders and down her back in shining, deep sensuous waves. She had changed for lunch, as had he. Now she was wearing a blue T-shirt with a silver designer logo on the front. The clingy fabric drew his eyes to the delicate shape of her high breasts.

"They've been here for thousands of years," she was saying, snapping him back to attention, "but they came from South East Asia originally, where they must have been domestic dogs. Over the four or five thousand years they've been here, they've established themselves in the wilds. They're our number-one predator. They can attack, even kill—especially if the victim is small, like a child."

"One doesn't like to think of that," he said gravely. "What about sheep? Mature cattle would be able to fend them off, surely?" He was frowning slightly.

"Not the calves. The alpha male is especially dangerous. So is the alpha female. They hunt in packs. We don't have the Great Wall of China, but we do have the longest man-made fence in the world."

He was quick to reply. "I have heard of the famous Dingo Fence."

"We'll take you to see Kooraki's section of it before you go home," she offered.

Even thinking of his departure gave her a distinct wrench. That only added to her sense of unreality. Who could expect to be so susceptible in such a very short time? She had to be aware her sense of trepidation was spiced with undeniable excitement. She only hoped he wasn't witness to it.

"The Dingo Fence is close to six thousand kilometres long," she carried on, her tone rather clipped. "It was shortened from well over eight thousand kilometres in 1980 because of the high repair costs. Six feet of wire mesh with steel and timber posts. It's a never-ending job maintaining it, but it protects over twenty-six million hectares of sheep and cattle grazing country. You're in trouble big-time if you forget to shut a gate."

"Who would know out here?" He waved a hand at the empty miles that ran for as far as the eye could see.

"You'd be surprised. Everyone keeps an eye out. Everyone knows if there are tourists or strangers in the area. Cattle-and-sheep men would never be guilty of such an offence."

He could see the jagged shape of the hills off to the north-west, their broken peaks and domes silhouetted against the cobalt-blue sky. The furnace-red of the earth made a wonderful contrast to the cloudless blue sky and the amazingly green trees and vegetation. The most beautiful tree he had seen along their route Ava had told him was the Outback's iconic Ghost Gum. It was easy to understand why. The tall upright tree with pendulous dark green leaves had a smooth, near blindingly white trunk and branches that made it glow in the sunlight. Even the distant hills were changing colour from brown to an orange that deepened into the red of the earth.

"You can stop here," Ava said as they arrived near the foot of a tumbling white waterfall.

Once out of the Jeep they could hear the loud murmur of the waters and their splash into the circular pool. A surprising amount of water was falling into it.

Varo moved closer, looking down into the depths. The silvered mirror-like surface threw back his own reflection. That too of the beautiful blonde Ava, who stood at his shoulder like an ethereal vision.

"It's so hot. A swim would be most welcome." He turned to her, the movement of his wide shoulders causing a flutter of air to cross the pool and form ripples.

"Bathing suits optional?" The coolness of her voice was intended not to give her inner turmoil away.

"You don't think it the duty of a good hostess to—"

"Varo, I know you're teasing," she protested, looking up into his brilliant mocking eyes.

"Even if you're really tempted?" He seemed to be towering over her. "The water is crystal-clear." He bent to dip a hand into it. "And so refreshingly cool."

"Varo, I'm getting a little nervous around you," Ava murmured.

He straightened. "You are *very* safe with me."

"I know that," she said hurriedly. "You also know what I mean. If you want a swim we have many lagoons. Dev, Amelia and I spend countless hours swimming in our favourite lagoon, the Half-Moon. The most gorgeous water lilies on the station grow there—the sacred blue lotus. They decorate the perimeter, along with all the water reeds. The lagoon is very deep in the middle. One day you can swim there. Maybe have a picnic."

"With you?" He fixed his dark eyes on her.

"Maybe," she said, half turning away.

"Maravillosa!" He had an instant vision of her, naked

as a water nymph, her long golden hair cascading over her shoulders, her beautiful skin with the lustre of a pearl.

Ava, for her part, was glad of her gift for composure—even if it was being giving an almighty workout. She pointed upwards, a pulse beating in her throat. "There's a big cave up there that goes so far back into the hills I used to be terrified I would get lost if I ventured too far. See, Varo?" She glanced at him, only to find him looking at her. "It's the one partially camouflaged by those feathery sprays of acacia. You'll have to duck your head at the entrance, but the interior at the central point is over two metres high."

"The roof has never caved in on anyone?" he asked, beginning to stare upwards.

Ava gave a little shudder. "Never. But I didn't dare to venture into the cave's recesses like Dev. Even Mel was scared. We have a famous mystery novel called *Picnic at Hanging Rock,* written by Joan Lindsay. It was made into a film way back in the 1970s. It tells the story of the disappearance of several schoolgirls and their teacher during a picnic at Hanging Rock on St Valentine's Day. The book is in our library at home. I've read and re-read it. It's a haunting tale. The missing party was never found."

"You think you will disappear as well?" he asked in teasing fashion.

"Wait until you're inside the cave," she replied, her composure regained.

"You think I'll get cold feet?"

"Laugh all you like." She gave him a sparkling look that was like a brief taunt. "I've known visitors to our great desert monuments, the aboriginal sacred sites Uluru and Kata Tjuta, come away stunned by the atmosphere. Why, some find the Valley of the Winds at Kata Tjuta very scary—especially when the winds are blowing. It's another world."

"One I intend to visit." He put out his elegant tanned hand. "Let me help you."

His wonderfully expressive voice sounded so tender her heart shook. She had no recourse but to put her hand in his, feeling his long fingers close around hers. She had known from the start nothing was going to be *normal* with this man. The suppressed excitement, the assault on her senses was way out of her experience. She had not dreamed of anything like this.

Together they climbed. A rock wallaby, startled by the approach of two figures, bounded back down the steep slope, making short work of reaching the bottom. Once when Ava's foothold slipped Vero gathered her close, wrapping one arm around her. She gave an involuntary little cry. She knew it wasn't fright. It was something far more dangerous that had her catching her breath.

At that height the rumbling of the waterfall was much louder. Big splashes fell over them—not enough to soak on such a hot day, but having a wonderful effect. Ava found herself taking droplets of cold water into her dry mouth. She wondered if this was how Amelia felt with Dev. There was a palpable ache inside her. It was sexual.

Gradually the footholds became narrower, but she turned her feet sideways just as she had done as a child. Varo might have been an experienced rock climber for all the trouble *he* was having. For all she knew he might have made an attempt on Mount Everest at one time. His own majestic Andes were close by his *estancia*, with a splendour rivalling the Himalayas.

In a final burst they reached the top, both of them turning to stare down at the infinite plains that spread out to the horizon. Not a single cloud broke up the dazzling peacock-blue of the sky.

"This is magic!" Varo exclaimed. "Superb!"

He still kept an arm around her. Maybe he had forgotten?

"And there's much more to see." She broke contact, restless and madly energetic. She might have caught fire from him. "Keep your head down until I tell you to lift it," she warned, preparing to enter the cave first.

In their shared childhood she, Dev and Amelia had always brought torches so they could explore inside. On a fairly recent climb she and Dev had left a lantern behind. When lit, it threw a very satisfactory light over the interior.

Varo reached out to pull away the curtain of vines that wreathed the neck of the cave.

"It's dark inside," she said over her shoulder. "Don't forget to keep your head down."

He nodded. He had no need to be told. In actual fact he had kept right behind her, to catch her should she slip on all the loose pebbles as fine as gravel.

Then the plunge into the tunnel!

It wasn't as dark as he'd expected. Although no ray of blazing sunshine pierced the cave, it still managed to cast a luminescence. He was able to judge the moment to stand erect. He saw her kneeling on the ground near one wall of the great tunnel, then there was suddenly light. Golden light that lit the cave and danced over the sandstone walls.

Varo stood mesmerised, his eyes tracking the images of the primitive art gallery. Even Ava, who had been inside the cave many times, stood rapt. More than anything she wanted their guest to be stirred and fascinated by what he saw. Varo moved closer to inspect one smooth, clean wall of the great cavern. It was dominated by a highly stylised drawing of a great serpent—a python—executed in chalky white with dark bands encircling the body and a black neck and head. The powerful reptile wound its sinuous body around two sides of the cave, its head high on the rock ceiling.

Evidently the great serpent was an important, even sacred creature from the aboriginal Dreamtime. Human figures with white circled eyes were represented only in stick-like form. The female forms with pendulous breasts. There were animals—kangaroos, emus—trees, and flocks of birds radiating over the walls, but what was most incredible, just as Ava had told him, was an outstanding drawing of a *crocodile*. It was surrounded by what could only be tropical palms. Fish too were represented, and what appeared to be turtles. Human handprints acted like a giant frame.

He turned back to Ava, who was watching his expression and trying to gauge his reaction. "This has to be a significant site!" he exclaimed. "Quite extraordinary."

"It is," she confirmed, "but very few people get to see it. It's not a sacred site, but it has to be protected. That's *our* job."

"Then I'm honoured. Thank you for bringing me here." He resumed his tour of the gallery, taking his time. As he walked he talked about the Inca civilisation of Peru, and the culture that had been shattered by the cruel and bloody Spanish Conquest. "Ancient temples and tombs were pillaged by the Conquisadors. Gold and silver booty to enrich the coffers of the Spanish Crown. In return Catholicism was forced on them."

"Your family is Catholic?"

He shrugged without answering.

"I've often wanted to visit South America," she said. "Especially since Dev came home filled with the marvels of your world. You were the one who took him to Machu Picchu?"

"Ah, yes—the secret cloud-shrouded ceremonial city of ancient Peru. That vast empire included the north-west of Argentina. Machu Picchu is one of the must-see places one should visit before one dies, Ava. Anyway, when you come to Argentina it will be my privilege to show you all we can offer." He turned suddenly, bending his dark head so he could whisper softly in her ear. "I'll even teach you how to dance the tango."

"Of which you are a master?" She felt the flush rise to her face.

"Of course."

It was so quiet inside the cave it was almost as though they were in some ancient cathedral, cut off from the rest of the world.

Varo was looking at the tunnel that led off the main cavern and went as far as anyone knew back deep into the eroded hills. It appeared as if he were debating whether it was wise to explore it.

"*No,* Varo!" she found herself exclaiming. "No one has ever mapped any of the passageways. No one even knows if there are exits. You're not Indiana Jones."

He turned back. The brilliant dark glance that swept over her was amused. "Maybe not. But I have been in some very scary places—including the South Pole. You're frightened I might want to explore in there?"

"I'm frightened I might lose you," she said.

"That won't ever happen."

It was said so gently, yet Ava thought she would remember his expression for as long as she lived. "We *must* go," she implored. "Back into the sunlight."

"We've only just arrived. You realise this would probably lead to a whole cave system?"

"The hill country is honeycombed with them," she admitted. "But even Dev backed off after he had gone a good distance. In some places there's only crawling space. I have to tell you I'm a bit claustrophobic." She wrapped her arms around herself as though she were cold.

He remained quite still, not making any move towards

her. "There's no reason to be frightened, Ava," he assured her, his voice pitched low.

"I'm not frightened. I'm more *worried*."

He gave her a slight and dangerous smile. "That you'll find yourself lost?" Now he made a move towards her, extending his hand to lift her face to him. "You fight the attraction?"

It was so strangely quiet she could hear her blood whooshing through her veins. "What attraction?" Unnerved, she tried to deny the obvious.

"*Our* attraction," he said. "You think it inevitable I might want to kiss you?"

"Don't, Varo," she whispered, shaking her head. This man could mesmerise her.

"One moment in time," he coaxed. "It occurs to me you are suffering in some way."

"I've had years of it." She hadn't intended to say it, but she had.

"Then you need a new start."

Just like that.

The note in his voice sent her head spinning. She felt herself sway towards him even before he gathered her into his arms in a way no man had gathered her to him before. She couldn't move away. She didn't want to move away. Why she was allowing this she didn't want to understand. She should feel daunted. Their instant connection was near incomprehensible. Yet every last little thing about him was proving an intoxicant. Even the cool air inside the cave was aromatic with the scents of the wild bush.

"I love that mouth of yours," he muttered, his handsome head poised over hers. "A man might only dream of kissing it." He touched her lower lip with the pad of one finger, effectively opening up her mouth to him.

That ignited such a response inside her she feared her

heart might stop. She was desperate for this, but all the while she felt deeply perturbed. From here on she was in his power. Yet she didn't push away, or ask him to stop. She knew he would if she did. Only right at that moment she knew this was what she wanted. She *had* to have it before she let go.

He was kissing her, tasting her, cupping her face with strong but exquisitely gentle hands. He kissed her not once but over and over, each time more fully, more deeply. A thousand brilliant stars were bursting behind her closed eyelids. Her hands had come up to clutch at his shirt, bunching it, her long nails maybe even hurting him if they pierced the fine cotton. This was longing, *desire*, on a grand scale, and the sensation was worth anything. She was far, far more vulnerable than she could ever have imagined. A near stranger had taken her captive when her husband had never succeeded in even pushing her to a climax.

He didn't stop. Perhaps he couldn't. If so, neither could she. She was utterly bewitched. He would have already identified that. He understood the power of the flesh would be too great. Ava felt as though her bones were dissolving, her flesh melting, yet the delta of her body felt oddly *heavy*. One of his hands was hard at her arched back. The other swept over her breast. Her nipples were standing erect with the height of arousal that was in her. His every action, so masterful, demolished all coherent thought. She felt in another moment they would sink onto their knees before falling back on the sand. Neither of them stopping. Neither of them prepared to try.

You've got to fight out of this delirium.

Her inner voice was crying out to her, desperate for her to listen. This could turn out to be a bitter, very traumatic mistake.

Make yourself care. No matter what you feel, this could come back to haunt you.

Her eyes flew open, coming slowly into focus, though she still felt bound to him.

For an instant Varo felt profoundly disorientated. Then he realised it was her soft moan that had forced him back to reality, back to control. He hadn't been able to get enough of her. The pressure on him had been unrelenting. Never in his life had he wanted a woman more. Locked in his arms, she'd seemed to him to be the very image of man's one great desire. But it was all so very complicated. This beautiful woman was still married—however unhappily. She was the much loved sister of his friend. He was a guest on Kooraki.

He told himself all this as he fought down the tumult inside him. Without thinking he raised a hand to brush her tumbling cascade of golden hair away from her face and over her shoulders. "There's no point in denying attraction, Ava," he said quietly. "Your life is complicated at the moment, but I can't think kissing you was a mistake."

"A woman is to be enjoyed?" she asked, brittle-voiced. Her tone was far sharper and more cynical than she'd intended.

There was a hush before he answered. "Do not demean the moment, Ava. Come, let's go back into the light."

She caught his arm as he started to turn away. "Forgive me, Varo. I didn't mean that the way it came out. I'd given up feeling—" She broke off.

"Did you love your husband at all?" He stared down into her eyes.

"If you had asked me back then I would have claimed I did."

"But he loved you? He continues to love you?"

The air around them seemed to be trembling. "Leave it there, Varo," she advised. "You know nothing about it."

His dark, handsome features tautened. "I know you want an escape."

"What else should I do?" she burst out with too much emotion. "Come on, tell me. Stay in a loveless marriage?"

"On *your* side," he pointed out.

"So judgemental?" Now there was an immeasurable distance between them. She might have known. "With your strict moral code I'm shocked you resorted to kissing me. Me—a married woman!"

He shrugged a wide shoulder. "Maybe I've been possessed, enchanted, bewitched…whatever. Temptation clings to you like a diaphanous veil. You're a very beautiful woman, Ava. Surely there have been other men in your life?"

"Irrelevant!" she said, with a downward chop of her hand. "Let's think of this as a summer storm. Over as quickly as it began."

Except it wasn't over. They both knew that.

CHAPTER FOUR

AVA spent a sleepless night. Never for a moment could she get Juan-Varo de Montalvo out of her mind. He might have been sleeping alongside her, so palpable was his aura. The power he had over her had arisen on its own. She hadn't invited it. Her conscience was clear on that point. Neither had she planned it.

It was some comfort to realise he too had surrendered to the massive force that had reached out for them and held them fast. The electrical charge that flowed between them was mutual. What had happened—and really were stolen kisses so illicit?—had caught him up too. He had not persisted when he heard her involuntary little moans. He had swiftly drawn back, only to brush back the wild mane of hair that had tumbled all around her face, with golden skeins clinging to the skin of his face and his neck.

But, *oh!* She had never known a kiss could make one's heart rise like a lark. It had been so unbelievable to take wing. She thought she would always be able to recall that weightless feeling, the shooting stars behind her eyes. Why hadn't Luke kissed her like that?

He didn't know how. He simply wasn't capable.

Yet she had been faithful to him. She wasn't the sort of woman who indulged in meaningless flings. Until now. If one could call rapturous kisses infidelity. For the first time all thoughts of Luke blurred. It was the past. Luke would move on.

Or so she believed.

Dev flew in around noon, with his bride-to-be Amelia and their parents, Erik and Elizabeth, for so long estranged, now back together again, and looking happy and wonderfully fit after a trip to beautiful Tasmania. There were three other passengers, all Devereaux relatives, including her cousin Karen.

Karen's parents were supremely self-assured people, partners in a blue chip law firm, and Karen too was a very confident, good-looking young woman, but remarkably exacting—almost driven, to Ava's mind. Two years older than Ava, she had always adopted a patronising attitude towards her younger Langdon cousin. There was plenty of money in the family. Like her, Karen had no need to work, but Karen was in fact a successful interior designer of the minimalist style. Whenever she stayed at Kooraki she had a habit of mooching around the handsomely decorated rooms—so many collectors in the family—as though she'd like to clear the lot out and start again.

Surely that would be like obliterating the past? In any case Kooraki was the Langdon stronghold. She remembered her grandfather referring to Karen as "that very unpleasant girl."

Thank God for Amelia, Ava thought as she hugged her. Amelia was a kindred spirit—the sister she'd never had and now would.

Karen locked on to Juan-Varo de Montalvo the instant her startled dark eyes fell on him. If expressions were anything to go on their Argentine guest had come as an enormous surprise. Indeed, her mouth fell half open as if in shock. Ava even thought she heard a gasp.

How fantastic was this!

They were all assembled in the Great Hall, with Dev making introductions.

Varo had no difficulty in recognising what qualities his friend Dev saw in his bride-to-be. Not only was Amelia beautiful in the Italianate fashion—large, lustrous dark eyes, lovely olive skin and wonderful thick dark hair—her manner would always draw people to her. As far as he was concerned she suited Dev perfectly. The Devereaux relatives, however, were quite different from the warm and friendly Langdons. They acted as though they owned the earth, their manner, to Varo's mind, almost ridiculously regal. Same with the daughter, Karen.

She was much too thin for her height, but graceful, with a long elegant neck, good bones, long almond-shaped brown eyes, and glossy dark hair cut in a bob with a deep fringe to draw attention to her unusual eyes. She was dressed from head to toe in black. Skin-tight black jeans, black T-shirt with a white logo, black high-heeled boots. She stood staring at him with such intensity she might have been testing to see if he were real.

All three Devereauxes, he thought, were surprisingly *arrogant*. He had to use that word—but on the basis of what? Having money and a position in society appeared to be an end in itself. Dev, his beautiful Amelia and of course Ava displayed no such characteristic, and they were the ones with the *real* money and a fantastic ancestral home.

Ava had the job of escorting her relatives upstairs. Her mother and father headed off to their old suite of rooms. Natalie Devereaux nodded her approval of the guest room with its adjoining *en suite* bathroom. Mercifully it would do. Karen stalked ahead to her room, just down the hallway, turning on Ava the minute they were inside the door.

"Why on earth didn't you tell me that man was going to be here?" she demanded, her brown gaze snapping so sharply it could drill holes.

Ava took her time to answer. "That man?" she queried gently.

"De Montalvo," Karen said with a frown. "Oh, for God's sake, Ava, don't play silly games. He's *gorgeous*!"

"Much too *masculine* for gorgeous, don't you think?"

Karen ignored her cousin as though her opinions were of little importance. "I've never seen such a stunning-looking man. And that voice! God, it nearly melted my bones. He is no doubt rich?" She shot Ava another piercing look. "Any Argentine of that class means rich."

"Varo's *parents* are rich," Ava offered mildly. She didn't add that Varo's mother was an American heiress.

"How long has he been here?" Karen continued her interrogation in an accusatory voice.

"Why do you ask?" Ava took a moment to push a beautifully scented pale apricot rose further into its copper bowl. Pal Joey, she recognised.

"Well, you will have been *alone* here, wouldn't you? With Dev in Sydney?" Karen opened her narrow eyes wide.

Ava's smile was amused. "I promise you, Karen, we didn't indulge in wild sex."

"As though you could!" said Karen, and threw her a pitying look. "You still have that virginal look, Ava. You must know that. How's the divorce going, by the way?"

Ava allowed herself a sigh. Karen never had been a sympathetic person. In fact Karen had given her rather a bad time of it when they were both at boarding school. It was Amelia who had always come to her rescue—like a protective big sister.

"Luke has been...*difficult*," she confessed. She didn't

mention the threatening letters and e-mails. "He believes it's my clear duty to go back to him."

"Well, he's a lovely man!" Karen said, on a wave of disapproval.

That hurt. Was Karen deliberately trying to hurt her? "What would you know about it?" Ava countered. "All he ever did was butter you up." The more over the top the compliment, the more Karen had swallowed it.

"He never *did*!" Karen protested, clearly outraged.

"The compliments were so thick you could eat them," Ava said. It suddenly struck her that Karen would have made a far more suitable bride for Luke than ever she had. "Maybe it's better if we don't talk about Luke."

"Especially as he's not here to defend himself," Karen huffed. "No, let's talk about Juan-Varo de Montalvo." Karen took a seat on the antique chest at the end of the four-poster bed. "He's not married? If he were his wife would have been invited."

"Of course. No, he's not married—but I would think he has legions of adoring admirers."

"South American women *are* very beautiful," Karen said, nibbling hard on her lower lip. "Where have you got him?" She fastened her eyes on her cousin.

"Got him?" Ava was rather enjoying acting dumb.

Karen shook her head so vigorously her thick fringe lifted off her smooth forehead. "Okay, you're having a little joke. Which one of the guest rooms is his?"

"You plan to drop in on him?" Ava lifted a delicate brow.

Karen leaned back on her hands. "No need. Are you sure *you* know what you're doing, cousin?"

"Meaning?" Ava's tone took on a surprising briskness.

"Maybe you should take care?" Karen cautioned. "Luke wouldn't like to hear you were alone in Kooraki with the sexiest man on earth."

"Is this a way of threatening me?" Ava held herself very still. "You plan to tell him?" Her years of tolerating Karen appeared abruptly over.

Karen must have grasped that fact—if not in its entirety. "Don't get me wrong, Ava. I've tried to keep a cousinly eye on you all our lives. I'm a real softie that way."

"What a pity I never realised that," Ava said, making a decision to leave before Karen upset her further. That was her style. "I'll leave you to unpack. Lunch at one."

Karen rose languidly to her feet, her legs as long and thin as a crane's. "When is he leaving?" she called.

Ava turned about. "Whenever he wants. He's most welcome to stay. He's our guest, Karen. He's come a long way."

Karen wasn't finished with her questions. "But after the wedding?" She moved abruptly towards Ava. "After Dev leaves on his honeymoon?"

"Dev won't be going on his own," Ava reminded her, not holding back on the sarcasm.

Karen scowled. "Does she *know* how lucky she is to get him—what with that mother of hers?"

Her cousin was on dangerous ground. "I'm astonished you haven't got the message, Karen," Ava said. "Dev is madly in love with Amelia. He's loved her since childhood. If I were you I wouldn't bring up the subject of Sarina Norton. In a very short time Amelia will be mistress of Kooraki."

"Never liked Amelia," Karen muttered.

"I well remember. She always did get the better of you. So heed my warning. Amelia and her mother are off limits."

Karen, a confident horsewoman, threw up her hands as though to quieten a fractious horse. "Yo, cousin!" she cried. "Yo! We're *family*. Surely we can have a private chat?"

"Certainly. Only you must remember Amelia is family too. I'm absolutely delighted to have her as a sister."

Karen quickly mustered some common sense. "She'll make a beautiful bride," she admitted, trying not to show her long-standing jealousy of the luscious Amelia. "I can see that. I'd let you see my own outfit, only it's going to be a big surprise. I had thought Amelia would ask me to be one of her bridesmaids. I mean we *did* go to school together."

Sometimes the clever Karen could be remarkably obtuse. "Be glad you were invited," Ava said, waggling her fingers. "See you soon."

"Can't wait for the polo match!" Karen called, a lift in her voice. "I have another outfit planned."

"Bet it cost plenty." Karen hardly wore the same outfit twice.

"Around a thousand bucks," she answered casually.

Ava closed the door after her. So Karen was going to spend her time trying to capture Varo's attention? At least she was a free agent, and she could be charming when she chose to be.

There was no reason to think Varo wouldn't respond. What she and Varo had shared had been a kind of enchantment—a surrender to an overpowering sexual desire. There were different words for it. Love was a long, long way from that.

The days flew, with everyone in high good spirits. Karen seemed to be laughing from dawn to dusk, changing several times a day, and all the while skipping around with Dev and Varo, as enthusiastic as a teenager, accompanying them on all their tours of the station. Or as many times as Dev allowed, being well aware where his cousin's interests lay.

"She's got it bad!" Amelia breathed softly in Ava's ear as Karen hurried out through the front door to join the men.

"She told me she thinks Varo is as magnificent as a black panther." Amelia paused a moment. "Actually, he *is*." She pulled a comical face. "A paragon of masculinity!"

They both laughed.

"It seems to me that if his eye is anywhere it's on *you*, Ava," Amelia continued shrewdly.

"Varo enjoys women," Ava said, glad her long hair was partially obscuring her expression. "Anyway I can't look at anyone—even someone who puts Karen in mind of a black panther—until my divorce is final."

"I wouldn't be *too* scrupulous," Amelia advised. "Luke doesn't deserve it."

"I know. He wants me back."

"Of course he does!" Amelia exclaimed, no admirer of Ava's weak, excessively vain husband. "You're a prize. He's stupid enough to think once he has you back again he can continue to control you."

"That's not going to happen." Ava sounded very firm. "It's just taking a while for it to sink in."

"He contacted me, you know," Amelia confessed after a considered moment.

"What? Just recently?" Ava struggled not to show her anger.

"Before we came away. He's a desperate man. We spotted him at a reception. He says he loves you. He adores you. If this divorce goes through it will destroy him."

"What did you say?"

"Exactly what you'd expect. I told him it was over. Dev and I think he was one lousy husband. Not worthy of you. It's his colossal pride that's hurt, Ava."

"No one knows that better than I," Ava murmured, checking a pang of regret for what might have been. "Let's go for a swim," she suggested.

"Good idea!" Amelia swiftly agreed. She stood up, glowing with health and energy. A woman on the eve of marrying her one true love. "Half-Moon?"

Karen usually spent time in the homestead's swimming pool, doing endless laps up and down. No matter how thin she was Karen thought she could be thinner. It was impossible to change her mindset.

"Half-Moon it is."

In the heat they took one of the station vehicles to the lagoon, where the silvery-blue heatwaves were throwing up their fascinating illusions. They might have been lost in the mirage.

Amelia parked at the top of the slope leading down to their favourite lagoon. She was wearing a black nylon-Spandex one-piece that fitted her beautiful body with its hourglass curves like a glove. Ava had chosen one of the four bikinis she kept in her closet. Spandex top and bottom, its colours were a mix of ocean hues—cobalt, emerald and aquamarine.

They raced across the sand, leaving their things in a heap and moving to the water's edge. As always the perimeter was decorated with exquisite blue lotus lilies.

Amelia turned with a smile. "All right, let's get it over!" she challenged.

Both knew the water would offer a shock of cold in the golden heat of the day. With a cheer Amelia waded into the shallows that quickly fell away to the deep, but Ava, always fleet of foot, beat her into a dive. It sent up glittering arcs of spray that fell back into the lagoon. Ava was actually the better swimmer of the two, but built for speed not stamina.

After their invigorating swim they padded back up onto the pale ochre sand, patting themselves dry before spreading out their towels. They had moved back so all their faces and bodies received of the sunshine was a dappled light through the overhang of trees. Amelia, with her olive skin, tanned easily, but she wasn't after a tan for her wedding day. And Ava had always had to protect her "lily-white" skin. As Amelia's chief bridesmaid she wanted to look her best.

As they lay there, eyes closed, they discussed all aspects of the big day. Dev and Amelia were to honeymoon in some of the great cities of the world—London, Paris, Rome—before jetting off to the U.S.A. New York first, then San Francisco, before returning home. Two months in all. It wasn't either one's first time in any of those cities, but this time they would be together as man and wife.

"It will be so *exciting*!" Amelia breathed, suddenly pulling herself up to lean on one elbow and looking back over her shoulder. "Looks like we're having visitors."

Her beautiful face was vivid with delight. Amelia and Dev were every inch and for all time passionate about each other.

Ava sat up very quickly her heart giving a rhythmic jolt as she turned her head in the same direction.

"Look—it's Dev and Varo." Amelia sprang, laughing, to her feet. She looked gloriously happy. "Karen too." A dryness entered her tone.

Ava, however, was pierced by embarrassment. Always comfortable in a swimsuit—she was very slender without being bone-thin like Karen—she suddenly felt a strange panic that Varo's eyes would be on her. She didn't want that. She wanted to keep calm. She knew she was being foolish, but there it was. She could hardly reach for the sarong she had draped around her hips. That would be too obvious a cover-up. Instead she waved a hand as Amelia moved to greet the new arrivals.

She stood up, paused a moment, then headed back into the water as if wanting to cool off on this steamy hot day. Maybe they would be gone before she emerged? She knew she was acting like an overly shy and modest schoolgirl, but she felt incredibly self-aware around Varo. She was actually shivering a little in reaction. She had so little experience of the powerfully sexual. Luke had never been a turn-on, she fully realised.

When she came up, blinking the lagoon water out of her eyes and off her lashes, she saw with a kind of dismay the party of riders were stripping off, obviously intent on cooling off in the crystal-clear water.

"Oh, my God!" Her breath whistled between her teeth. They were coming in.

Dev and Varo had stripped to dark-coloured swimming briefs. Karen had exposed her ultra-thin body in a postbox-red one-piece with a halter neck. She stood at the water's edge, squealing at the cold as she put a toe in. She didn't even bend to splash her face. No preliminaries to accustom herself to the cold water. Both men charged past her like young gods, diving in unison into the water. Amelia was still at the water's edge, perhaps saying a few coaxing words to Karen, who now had her long arms criss-crossed over her body. Ava began to wonder if her cousin would come in at all.

There was a flat rock platform on the other side of the lagoon. It overhung the emerald-green waters by two or three feet. As children they had often used it as a diving board. She, Dev and Amelia had often sat there to sunbake and be alone. Now she struck out for the platform, proposing to sit there for a short time while the others took their refreshing dip. Dev always had pressing things to do. She would wait it out.

Amelia had joined Dev now, continuing the little rituals of childhood, diving under the water and chasing after each other like a pair of dolphins. Karen had evidently decided the water was too cold for her liking. She had retreated to the shade of the trees, keeping a keen eye on them all. Especially Varo.

He was a born athlete. Ava *knew* he was going to swim over to her. She knew for sure.

He did, his teeth flashing white in his handsome dark face, his skin pearled with drops of water.

"So, I always suspected you were half-mermaid," he mocked. "All you need is a circlet of sparkling crystals and emeralds around your blonde head. You need nothing else. Not even the covering of a swimsuit, however brief." With one lithe movement he hauled himself onto the platform. A trained gymnast couldn't have done it better. "You took one look at me and swam away," he accused her. "You should have been swimming *towards* me, don't you think?"

Now his lustrous dark eyes settled on her, touching every part of her body: Her long wet hair, drying out in the warm air, over one shoulder and down her back, her face, her throat, her breasts, taut midriff, slender legs. All was exposed to his eyes.

"Ava," he said, very gently.

She managed a soft reply. "Yes?"

"Nothing. I'm just saying your name."

She loved the way he said it. Unlike anyone else. There was that tension again. The high, humming *thrum* of sexual energy. He had a superb body, evenly tanned, no betraying untanned skin below his waist above the line of his black swimming trunks. The sun had hit everywhere. He was bronze all over. Totally unselfconscious. Unlike her.

"It is very clear to me, Ava, that you are avoiding me." There was a glinting sardonic look in the depths of his dark eyes.

He shocked her by leaning over to brush her bare shoulder with his mouth, licking up the few remaining sparkling droplets and taking them into his mouth.

"Varo!" She tried to move, her little cry blending with the call of a bird.

"You fear someone is watching?" he asked. "Dev and his beautiful Amelia are totally engrossed in each other, as it should be. It is only your cousin who has the binoculars trained on us."

"Surely not?"

"A joke," he teased. "Though I am quite sure if she had a pair handy we would be in her sights." His voice took on an amused note. "She is very jealous of you, is she not?"

Ava turned her head all the way to him, her expression one of actual disbelief. "Of course she isn't."

His look seemed to say he knew more about her than she would ever know herself. "I think she *is*. Why are you so nervous of me? It's perfectly natural for a man and a woman to sit and talk like this."

"I talk a lot easier when I'm wearing clothes," she confessed on a wry note.

He kept looking at her. "I want to touch you." His voice was low, so emotive he might have been exulting in his own desires. "I want to make love to you. I want to press kisses all over your body. I want to kiss you where you have never been kissed before." His hand moved so that his fingers closed over hers.

She felt a sharp, knife-like thrust deep in her womb, leaving a dull ache. "Why are we going with this, Varo?" she whispered, even with no one to hear.

"Isn't it obvious to you?" His fingers tightened. Very firm. He wasn't going to let her get away. "You have enchanted me."

She could barely answer. "I have made it clear I'm still married."

"You will soon have your freedom. That's what you want, isn't it?" He didn't tell her that her cousin, Karen, had sought to convince him Ava could have been the inspiration for *La Belle Dame sans Merci*. The memory of her words flooded back without prompt.

"Ava might look like vanilla ice cream, but I assure you she has another side," Karen had told him. "We call it the Langdon syndrome. They're tough people, the Langdons. Her husband, Luke, is a lovely man. He idolises her. Puts her on a pedestal. Such a terrible shame, but Ava didn't care to inhabit the role of wife. At least not for long."

Ava now turned to him, her eyes huge. "I shouldn't stay here."

"No," he murmured, his eyes lingering on her. "Your beautiful skin might get burned."

"I haven't *your* olive skin," she said defensively.

He lifted a hand to stroke the side of her neck. "Yours is as lustrous as a pearl. *'Full beautiful'* you are, Ava." He began to quote softly, dark and honey-tongued, "*'Her hair was long, her foot was light, and her eyes were wild.'*"

In truth he was the one doing the seducing, Ava thought. "I love Keats," she said on a surprised note. "Fancy your knowing that poem."

He shrugged. "A famous English poet, a famous poem. *La Belle Dame sans Merci.*"

"And I brought it to mind?" Was that how he saw her? Cool to cold? A little cruel?

He didn't answer. He fell back into the water and held up his arms. "Come here to me."

Little thrills of excitement were travelling the length of her spine. Yet she hesitated, aware Karen could see them. She was a cautious person, not at all adventurous, but it seemed her whole life was changing.

"Come," he repeated.

Her breath shook, but there nothing else she could do but allow herself to fall blindly into his outstretched arms.

They went under together. Down…down…into shimmering crystal depths shot through with rays from the sun. Varo held her body locked to his, as though she would never get away. His mouth pressed down with great ardour over hers. Surely this only happened in dreams? It was simply… *magic*.

But he was in need of more…a man held in captivity by an enchanting woman.

His hand had a life of its own. It plunged into her tiny bikini top, taking the weight of her delicate breast, the pleasure boundless. They were locked together so long Ava thought they might drown. She couldn't seem to care. Somehow this was not real. The moment was timeless. Locked together in the cool silvery-green depths yet burning with passion. This was a secret place of great beauty, the waters like silk against the skin. Best of all, they were far, far away from prying eyes.

They were moving to another stage. It was like a dreaming. They were weighted under water but not conscious of it. Only Varo, his strong arm locked around her, broke the idyll. They shot to the surface, faces turned up to the sky, both gasping for air. Dev and Amelia were lazily stroking their way back to them. Karen was standing right at the shoreline, one arm waving frantically, as though signalling to Ava and Varo to get out.

Ava knew she was in for a good talking-to. Karen hadn't been jealous of her before now. Her cousin had always acted like someone of elevated status—far superior to the younger Ava. She realised Karen had spent a lot of time trying to put her down, deflating any tendency towards a burgeoning self-confidence. Karen would be full of admonitions and she might even talk to Luke. Get in touch with him. Ava wouldn't put it past her. Karen was on Luke's side. She had no loyalty to Ava. She had to remember that. Karen could cause trouble.

Karen waited her moment until they were back at the homestead.

The men, Dev and Varo, refreshed, had returned to the Six Mile, where a thousand head of cattle were being yarded in advance of the road trains that were scheduled to arrive the following day.

Ava had taken a quick shower, washing the lagoon water out of her hair before changing into fresh clothes. She and Amelia planned on continuing their discussions with Nula Morris, the new housekeeper. Nula was a part aboriginal woman married to one of their best stockmen. Amelia's mother, the by now notorious Sarina Norton, had trained Nula as well as the rest of the domestic staff. She had done an extremely good job of it. No one could deny that.

Food and drink had to be planned for the coming polo weekend, and for the buffet at the party on Saturday night. For those who stayed on until Sunday, either camping out or finding a place in the station dorms, there would be a lavish Sunday brunch. All in all, the first big test for Nula—although she would have lots of help. The wedding reception, of course, would be fully catered.

Inevitably, Karen showed up at her door, charging past her. She spun to drill Ava with an accusatory look. Small wonder Amelia had long since christened Karen "The Snoop."

"You're spending a lot of time with Varo," she burst out, not beating about the bush.

Ava didn't hotly deny the allegation. Instead she said, very quietly, "Forgive me, but is that any of your business?" She was determined to hold on to her composure.

"Of course it is," her cousin hissed. "I've been looking out for you since we were kids. I never thought you capable of wayward impulses, Ava, but it seems you are. I believe I have the right as your cousin to point out that you've got your feet planted on the slippery slope." She stared at Ava intently, the pupils of her dark eyes black and huge.

"Which slope would that be?"

"Don't evade the issue, Ava."

"What? My wayward tendencies? You never stop, do you?" Ava sighed. "You have to show me you're far wiser, far more sophisticated than I. For years you were the superior schoolgirl. Now you're the experienced woman of the world. So far *you're* the one who has been chasing after our guest, Karen. We've all noticed."

Karen's face turned red. "Maybe a little," she confessed, trying to make light of it. "But *fun* is all it is," she maintained vigorously. "A bit of a release from my tight work schedule in the city. In any case, I'm a free agent. I have no commitment to anyone. Unlike *you*."

"And you can't help feeling a bit jealous?"

"Yo!" Karen did her extraordinary reining-in gesture. "Don't be so ridiculous! It has never occurred to me to be jealous of you, Ava. *Protective* is the word. We're cousins. Family. Right now you must be feeling very vulnerable. Don't think I can't see how easy it would be for you to fall for someone like Varo. Those dark eyes…the way he looks at a woman like she's the most desirable woman in the world. The smile. The charisma. It's all South American macho stuff. That's the way they are. Let me tell you, Varo is used to making conquests."

"I'm sure of it," Ava returned. "I can't think why you're working yourself up to such a state. Varo hasn't stolen my heart."

"Then *what*?" Karen demanded to know. "I'm a remarkably good judge and I'd say he has."

"I don't know if you're a good judge or not, but you're

remarkably interfering," Ava said. "You are my cousin, but you're also a guest here. I really don't need any lectures."

"Why take it like that?" Karen issued a protest. "Amelia has always carried on scandalously, so *she* won't advise you."

Ava's eyes sparkled dangerously. "I'd take that back, if I were you."

"Okay, okay—but Amelia is not you. Surely you recognise that? She's a very sensual woman. You're the Snow Maiden."

"I haven't been a maiden for years now, Karen. And I've told you before not to discuss or criticise Amelia or her mother. I consider Amelia my champion in all things. Not you."

"Well, then, make a fatal mistake!" Karen exclaimed, angry and affronted.

"Another one, you mean? You've shown far more loyalty to my husband than you've ever done to me."

"Why shouldn't I turn to Luke? He's my friend. He's a good man, Ava, and you've deliberately cast him aside. So much for your marriage vows. Luke loves you. Only now you've got all that money you want to be free."

Ava started walking to the door. "Maybe it's best if you leave now, Karen. You'd make a terrible marriage guidance counsellor. No one on the outside can see inside a marriage. If Luke considers himself unhappy, he made *me* unhappy for most of our married life. Like you, he took pleasure in putting me down, eroding my self-confidence."

Karen shook her glossy head. "I never remember him doing that. I strenuously deny it in my case. You're too thin-skinned, Ava. You take offence too easily. I didn't mean to upset you, but certain things have to be said. You know nothing about Juan-Varo de Montalvo beyond the fact he's Argentine, stunningly handsome, of good family and a splendid polo player. You're very beautiful, in your quiet way. It's nothing to him to start up a flirtation, even an affair. Ask him about the young woman he's left behind."

Ava couldn't ignore the stab of apprehension. "You know about such a woman?"

"I don't *know*," Karen replied in her familiar arrogant tone, "but I suspect it from a few things he's let drop. Think about it, Ava. He's nearly thirty years of age. His family will be expecting him to choose a bride soon. He wants a family. It's *time*. I wonder you haven't thought of all this. He's simply playing you for all it's worth."

"It's a wonder you haven't kept notes," Ava said, maintaining her cool. "Strange, I didn't think Varo had had the time, with you fussing over him, but thank you for your concern. If that's what it *is*. I would appreciate it if you kept all your insights to yourself for the rest of your stay. We Langdons want nothing to spoil this happy time. I could be mistaken—if so I'm sorry—but I think you're out to upset me."

Karen stalked to the door, her dark head held high. "I've simply told you what you need to know," she said sanctimoniously.

"You'll stay in touch with Luke?" Ava asked.

"Are you suggesting I don't?" Karen threw up her chin aggressively. "I'm not taking sides in this. I care for you both."

Ava ignored that spurious claim. "I'm sure he knows you're here. You both think you're in the perfect position to keep tabs on me."

"I'll forget you said that, Ava."

Ava took little heed of the tone of deep hurt.

"Better if you *remember* it," she replied.

CHAPTER FIVE

THE polo day was as brilliant as promised.

There was a great stir of excitement from the crowd as the Red Team, captained by James Devereaux Langdon, and the Blue Team, captained by the visiting Argentine Juan-Varo de Montalvo, cantered onto the field to wave upon wave of applause. Horses were part of Outback life, so it was no surprise polo was a great attraction, drawing crowds over long distances even by Outback standards. Polo was the fastest game in the world, and it had the seductive element of danger.

"Oh, isn't this *exciting*?" Moira O'Farrell, a very pretty redhead and a polo regular, threw back her head, rejoicing in the fact.

Four men to a team, all of them were tall, with great physiques and good-looking to boot, but all female eyes were on the Argentine. He was so *exotic*, so *out there*. Dev Langdon was taken, after all. No use looking to him. All these guys were seriously sexy. All at this point of time bachelors. That was of profound interest and concern. The polo "groupies" were among the most involved spectators. Would it be so amazing if one of them caught the eye of the devastatingly handsome Argentine? Not difficult to see oneself as mistress of some fabulously romantic *estancia* on the *pampas*.

Not to mention the high life in Buenos Aires, home of the dead-sexy tango.

In the main it had fallen to Ava to organise the weekend's events. Never one to sing her own praises—Ava was modest about her abilities—she actually had exceptional organisational skills. As her mother Elizabeth told her, with loving pride, "Far better than mine, my darling!"

Multi-coloured bunting decorated the grounds, aflutter in the light cooling breeze. Prominent amid the fluttering little flags was the Argentine, pale blue and white—Argentina was the polo capital of the world, a Mecca for top players—and the red, white and blue of Australia, a polo-playing nation. The polo field itself was a good three hundred yards in length and more than half that distance in width. Today, after concentrated maintenance, it was a near unprecedented velvety green. The going had to be just right for the game. Too hard would jar the legs of the polo ponies. Too soft would slow down the action.

Several of the players on the polo circuit had travelled overland with their string of ponies—though *ponies* was a traditional term. The polo ponies of today were full-sized horses, either thoroughbreds or thoroughbred crosses, their legs protected by polo wraps from below the knee to the fetlock. Long manes were roached, tails braided. Nothing could be allowed to snag the rider's mallet. The taller the horse, the longer the mallet. Both Dev and Varo were six-footers-plus.

Amelia was wearing a polka-dotted navy and white shirt, with chinos in bright red accentuating her long legs. There was no doubting which team Amelia was barracking for. Ava had found herself choosing a pale blue silk shirt to go with her white lightweight cotton jeans. No coincidence that her outfit bore the colours of the flag of Argentina. Karen wore dazzling white. Karen was always given to block colours. All black, all white, or all neutral beige. Once she had claimed she was channelling Coco Chanel. With some success, Ava had often thought. The tall, super-thin Karen always looked elegant. Today for the afternoon match she wore a collarless white shirt tucked into very narrow-legged white jeans with high heeled wedges on her feet. As a concession she had quite dashingly tied a blue silk scarf patterned in sun-yellow around her throat.

Behind her designer sunglasses Karen's dark eyes gleamed. She thought she was on to something. It wouldn't take her long to find the answers. She sat with the family— Erik and Elizabeth Langdon, Ava and Amelia the bride-to-be, and her own parents, who were giving the distinct impression they weren't all that keen on sport in general, and were apprehensive of such a dangerous sport as polo. For all they knew a charging player could lose control of his pony and plough into the area where they were sitting.

"You've done a great job, kiddo." Amelia complimented her friend and chief bridesmaid with real enthusiasm.

"I'm happy with it." Ava was watching Varo riding the bay gelding Caesar for the first chukka. The horse's hide had been lovingly burnished until it gleamed in the sunlight. Rider and polo pony looked magnificent. Out of the corner of her eye she saw Karen wave to Varo, as if he was her champion in a medieval joust. Ava transferred her gaze to her adored brother, who lifted a hand to them, then laughed as Amelia jumped to her feet waving a red bandana. Both young women laughed back in response. It was going to be a great day.

Ava had had the tall collapsible goalposts freshly painted in the colours of the two teams. Even the big white marquees that had been set up for food and drink had been decorated with the teams' colours. Adjacent picket fences had received a fresh coat of white paint.

The periods of play had already been decided. Six chukkas, each the traditional seven minutes long. Dev and Varo would only be playing two ponies, both well-trained Kooraki throughbred crosses. They had the right temperament, and proven speed, stamina and manoeuverability skills. Dev was used to all four ponies, and Varo had taken a hour or two to familiarise himself with his mounts' abilities.

Two members of Dev's team had brought along half a dozen good polo ponies between them, the idea being they could switch a tired pony for a fresh one between chukkas. Ava knew all the players. She had seen them play many times before, so she knew they were highly competitive. Dev's team, all from Outback properties, weren't going to let the Argentine's team win.

They were aiming high.

The best player on a team was usually the number three—the tactical leader and the most powerful hitter. Dev and Varo both wore a large white number three on the back of their coloured shirts, worn over the traditional fitted white breeches and glossy black riding boots. All players wore helmets with a chin strap. This was a dangerous game, with powerful young men wielding hardwood mallets.

"That's one sexy outfit!" Moira was really on a roll. She made the excited comment to the amusement of those around her.

It was a very friendly crowd, with lots of exchanges between spectators. Not that Moira wasn't spot on. Polo always attracted women who just happened to fancy the players more than the game.

It soon became evident that the number three players— the captains, the high-handicap players, hard-hitting, hard-riding, with an impressive armoury of strokes—were the best on the field. Neither was giving any quarter. In fact it was obvious to all the game's fans that the arrival of the dashing Argentine was proving a great stimulus to players and spectators alike.

It was a hard-played, hard-drawn contest, but in the end only one team could win. During the third chukka Tom McKinnon, number one on Dev's team, took a fall while covering the opposition number four. Tom swiftly and gamely remounted, but the Blue Team had gained the advantage. It was Varo who hit a magnificent winning goal that near stupefied the crowd so quickly and unexpectedly had it happened.

The Blue Team won, with good-natured cheers soaring to the cobalt-blue heavens.

It had been a wonderful match. The best for a very long time.

"Let's face it. The Argentine lifted the game. The captains were matched, but the others weren't in the same class."

It was Ava who was to present the cup to the captain of the winning team. Up close to Varo, she was perilously conscious of his sizzling energy, the sheer force of his sexual attraction that blazed like a brand. Indeed, to the crowd she looked like a beautiful and delicate porcelain figurine before him.

"Congratulations, Varo," she said sweetly, though the nerves in her body were leaping wildly. "That was a very exciting match."

"Gracias, señora," he said, silken suave, but with that mocking glint in his eyes. "I thoroughly enjoyed it." Bending his dark head, his hair as high-sheened as a bird's wing, he kissed one of her cheeks, and then the other,

breathing into her ear, "You look as cool as a camellia, *mi hermosa.*"

She knew her cheeks pinkened but she moved back smilingly to present him with the silver cup. It was no everyday sort of thing, and one he would be happy to take back to Argentina.

Fresh waves of applause broke out. The crowd had melted for the Argentine. He had such animal magnetism—like some wonderful exotic big cat. Everyone was basking in his physical exhilaration.

Dev joined them now, his hair as golden as Varo's was raven-black. He threw an arm around his friend's shoulder. "My team will make a comeback," he joked. "That was a great game, Varo. You inspired us all."

Not to be left out, Amelia made a move up to them. Dev caught her around the waist, his aquamarine eyes sparkling with health and vigour. Brother and sister side by side could have been twins, which had been remarked on since childhood.

"Let's get ourselves a cold drink," Dev said, and started to move off to a marquee.

Karen bit her lip hard. She wasn't going to be denied her moment. She followed them and caught Varo's arm firmly, causing him to swing about. "May I add my congratulations, Varo?" She brushed his cheek with her hand. "That was a splendid match," she told him with warm enthusiasm, tugging at her blue and yellow silk scarf with its Argentine flag colours.

Varo responded gallantly. "Thank you so much, Karen. I enjoyed it too."

"I'm sure every woman in the crowd was urging you on," Karen said archly. "I know Ava was." She transferred a pointed gaze to her cousin.

"Well, *partly*," Ava responded lightly. "I wanted Dev's

team to win at the same time. But as we all know there can only be one winner."

"And winner takes all!" Karen's tone was decidedly provocative.

"Why did we ever invite that woman?" Amelia asked Ava later.

"Beats me," Ava responded. "We're from different galaxies. But she's family. It doesn't always mean families are nice."

"She always was a pain in the neck," said Mel, giving Ava a hug. "Don't let her bug you. Obviously she's trying to. Jealous, I'd say."

Ava gave a little grimace. "You're the second person who's told me recently Karen is jealous of me."

"So are you convinced?" Mel asked with a quirked brow.

"Getting there," Ava admitted with a laugh.

"I bet it was Varo who made the comment," Mel said very softly in Ava's ear.

"In a word, *yes.*" Ava blushed.

Mel's lustrous dark eyes were fixed on her friend's face. "Both of you are playing it ultra cool, but it's not hard to see the attraction. It pulses around you. I'm sure you're aware Karen is keeping you under observation? To report to Luke, I wonder?"

Ava felt a hot prickling sensation all over her body. "There's nothing to report," she said huskily.

"You deserve to be happy, Ava," Mel said with the greatest affection. "Don't turn your back on your chances."

And so they came to the night of the party.

Ava knew she had far more in the way of formal eveningwear than most women. God knew she had attended any number of grand and boring balls, parties, fundraisers and other functions. She counted herself most fortunate in lots of ways. Not all. Luke had once sent her back upstairs to change one of her gowns because he had considered it not stunning enough. In actual fact it had been a designer outfit, purchased when she and her mother had been in Paris, the City of Light. It just went to prove Luke knew nothing about style and *haute couture*.

For tonight's party she chose the same full-length gown. Her mother had insisted on buying it for her because of its masterly cut and glorious colour. She knew Mel had a beautiful gold full-length gown, with bare shoulders and a richly embroidered top. Karen would be channelling Chanel again. Probably slinky black. Karen was forever quoting the infamous Wallis Simpson remark, "A woman can't be too rich or too thin." The other women guests would have brought something to dazzle. Every woman loved to dress up, and there weren't all that many occasions. When one arose they made the most of it.

Ava debated whether to pull her hair back or leave it loose. Men loved long hair. In her experience they considered it an unparalleled look for a woman. In the end she decided to go with movement. She did a little teasing to her thick gleaming locks, and even she thought the end result was very glamorous. It was party-time, after all. The satin gown in a lovely shade of purple hugged every curve, every line of her body. The bodice, ruched from below the bust, was held up by a shoestring halter with a long scarf-like pleat falling down the centre of the gown. Right now Ava felt as attractive as she could get.

For her twenty-first birthday her parents had given her a white-gold sapphire and diamond necklace, with matching sapphire and diamond drop earrings.

She realised what was happening. She was making herself as beautiful as possible for *one* man. Even thinking it brought out a rosy blush. Juan-Varo de Montalvo had had an enormous impact on her from the moment her eyes fell on him. Now she knew all about his powerful charm.

Turning about, she addressed her glowing reflection. "You've changed, Ava. You're almost a dual personality."

Cool, calm Ava and the woman who turned to flame in a near stranger's arms. A man, moreover, from another land.

For all she had lived life as a married woman, she had never felt remotely like this. She had never been in this intensely emotional state or felt such feverish excitement. And she was taking a huge gamble. One she might never win.

"It isn't like you at all," she told herself. "But it's magic!"

And how was it going to end? There were always consequences to actions.

On one side euphoria. On the other a certain trepidation which she sought to subdue but couldn't. She really knew very little about Varo. She could be playing with fire and she had always thought of herself as governed by cool logic. Falling madly in love was madness in its way. And she had a past. Some men didn't like a woman to have a past. Not to marry, anyway. Was it conceivable Varo could be regarding her in some way other than she believed? There was passion on both sides. Neither could deny that. But she would die of shame if he was only thinking of her in terms of a wild affair. How did she really know if he didn't have someone waiting for him at home? Now, *that* was logical. A man like Varo—a man of strong passions—surely would have a special woman tucked away. Karen had hinted at it. But Karen was not to be trusted. Karen only wanted to hurt her.

Momentarily her heart sank. Then she made the effort to throw off any negative feelings. She was like a woman who had been buried alive. Now she was going to enjoy herself. Enjoy life. She had been unhappy for such a long time. That had to change. She had to work at making her life change.

She wanted to be a stronger woman than she had ever been. It seemed to her this man who had come into her life, Juan-Varo de Montalvo, was helping her be just that. Her anxieties dissolved.

A few minutes later, looking supremely beautiful and composed, she made her way down the rear staircase to the kitchen, greeting Nula and her helpers with a warm smile. "Everything going okay?"

"All under control!" Nula assured her.

"Great!"

"You look absolutely beautiful!"

Nula spoke for all of them, charmed and delighted. Miss Ava, such a lovely, friendly person, had never been treated the way she should have been. The Old Man, Gregory Langdon, had been a genuine tyrant. Everyone on the station, family and employees alike, had taken a good deal of punishment from him. Miss Ava's husband—from the viewpoint of the staff, at least—wasn't half good enough for her. Good riddance, they all thought, now they knew Miss Ava was well into the process of divorcing him. She deserved and hopefully would find a far better man.

The party had already started. Music was playing through the house. All the exterior lights, and the lighting around the pool, the pool house and the landscaped gardens, were turned on, transforming the whole area into a fairyland. Couples were dancing in the Great Hall and out on the rear terrace. She had a good view of Dev, with his beautiful Amelia clasped in his arms. Her heart shook with love and gratitude. Everything at long last had turned out so splendidly for them. These were two individuals who had been made for each other. Wasn't that a source of wonder? Everything was so much better with Mel around. She found herself rejoicing that in one week's time Mel would become her sister-in-law—the sister she'd never had.

The instant she spotted the fabulous Argentine momentarily alone Moira O'Farrell broke away from her group, crossing the room swiftly to speak to him while she had the chance. Ava's cousin, the pretentious Karen Devereaux—so terribly hard-edged, wearing a very stylish black jersey dress—had actually unbent sufficiently to tell her Juan-Varo de Montalvo had picked *her*, Moira, out of the crowd.

"It's your wonderful red hair, darling," Karen had pointed out in a voice that hid insincerity. She really disliked red hair.

So he *had* noticed her! Moira had the sensation she was awakening to a dream. The Argentine was *gorgeous*, and Karen had let drop that he came from a fabulously wealthy family. Not only that, he was unattached. She didn't know if she believed that was true or not. How could such a man be unattached?

Well used to the ways of women, especially women dead set on chasing him, Varo was soon alerted to the redhead's intentions. She was very pretty, her small neat head a mass of silky curls, and she was wearing a lovely spring-green dress, but all he could think of was Ava and when she was going to appear.

The intensity of the feelings he had for his friend's sister was threatening to overwhelm him. He was always gentle with women, and tender too, he supposed, but he had never experienced such a potentially dangerous passion. He wanted her. Very, very badly. He had not been prepared for her. He wasn't one to fool around, treating women with a callous hand.

He had no idea where these feelings were going. Ava

was still married. He could not stay in Australia, despite the country's great appeal to him, the people, the way of life. He had to go home. He was his father's heir. He and his father had great plans. He might be able to grow to love Australia, especially the vast Outback, but a woman like Ava would be extremely unhappy away from her homeland. That was if her feelings even came remotely close to his own.

At the moment it was a dilemma. All of it. He cared too terribly much.

The redhead raced up to him, her face full of animation and, it had to be said, invitation. "Please, Varo, I'd love to dance—wouldn't you?"

She was so sweet, so openly flirtatious, he couldn't help but smile back at her. Very gallantly he took her arm, leading her out onto the terrace where everyone was in a rather *loving* dance mode.

"Fabulous party, Ava," one of the male guests said as she passed him. "You look glorious!"

Ava didn't reply, but she smiled and blew him a kiss. Invitations to join different groups were called to her as she made her way from the Great Hall into the living room, wondering all the while if Varo was out on the terrace. He was so tall, so much a stand-out figure, she would have spotted him easily had he been inside the house.

Easier still to spot him on the terrace. He was dancing with Moira O'Farrell. Moira's pretty face was uplifted to him, her expression one of almost delirious excitement.

Ava found herself standing perfectly still, her heart rocked by an unfamiliar pang of jealousy laced with an irrational sense of betrayal. Surely Varo could dance with whomever he pleased? He couldn't help being so devastatingly attractive to women. He appeared to be staring down into Moira's melting blue eyes. There was very little space between their bodies, although in height they were mis-matched. Varo's raven head was bent to hear what Moira was saying. Ava saw him smile—that beautiful white flash that lit up his polished bronze complexion. He would draw any woman and compel her to follow him.

Unnerved, inhaling quickly, breasts steeply rising, Ava turned back into the living room. She was caught by a sudden fear that Varo might be toying with her. Then she reminded herself she had always suffered from a lack of confidence.

About time you took trust as a maxim.

Some time later, someone suddenly and very precipi-tately bumped into her.

"Oh, for heaven's sake. I'm sorry, Ava." It was Moira O'Farrell doing the apologising.

From looking radiant, Moira now looked hectically flushed and, yes, distressed. What on earth had happened to cause such a change?

"That's okay, Moira," Ava said companionably. "You look like you're leaving?" She was half joking, half seri-ous. She put out a steadying hand. Moira was a guest.

"No, no. I'm having a marvellous time," Moira's protest had a touch of mild hysteria. "Look, I shouldn't say this, but that bitch of a cousin of yours, Karen Devereaux—" Moira broke off as though she'd suddenly realised to whom she was speaking.

"Whatever has she said to upset you?" Ava asked, star-ing into Moira's face. She took Moira's slender arm, mov-ing them away to a relatively quiet corner.

"It was unforgivable, really." Always chirpy, Moira now looked both downcast and angry.

"Sure you're not being over-sensitive?" Ava questioned.

"She's nothing like you!" Moira shook her head so vigorously her curls bounced. "I always thought she was a bit on the vicious side."

"*Tell* me, Moira," Ava insisted.

Moira's face contorted into a grimace. "She tried to make a fool of me. You'd better ask her."

"I'm asking *you*, Moira. I prefer to speak to you." Ava spoke firmly.

"All right!" Moira made her decision. "She told me Varo had picked me out of the crowd. Her very words. *Picked me out of the crowd.* The implication was he fancied me. Like a fool I believed her. Men *do* fancy me, as I expect you know. But obviously she was having a good laugh at my expense. I practically forced Varo to dance with me. Don't get me wrong. He's a great guy—a perfect gentleman, lovely manners, and a *super* dancer. Stupid me, pressing myself against him… I could die. But it seems he has a girl back home. Of course he would, wouldn't he? A drop-dead gorgeous guy like that. Oh, God, I feel such a fool." A sound like a hot rush of self-loathing escaped her.

"Why would you?" Ava tried hard to sound understanding. Indeed she *was*. But her own fearful thoughts were spinning out of control.

"Oh, Ava, I was so *obvious*," Moira wailed. "I was flirting with him for all I was worth."

Ava gathered herself. Her voice, miraculously, sounded nice and normal. "Nothing much wrong with that, Moira. If you look around, everyone is playing the flirting game. It's a party. Cheer up." There seemed little else she could say.

Varo has someone back home. He's admitted it. Moira wouldn't lie.

"I've never told you this before," said Moira, "but that smug cousin of yours is very jealous of you. I've wanted to tell you for a long time now. You're so lovely too." Moira's eyes were suddenly brimming with tears. "Just you be careful of her."

Ava lent forward and spontaneously kissed Moira's flushed cheek. "Come on, Moira. So Varo has a love interest at home? You can easily find one right here. Blink the tears away and go enjoy yourself. That's an order."

Moira lifted her head with smiling gratitude. "Thanks, Ava. You're an angel."

They parted company with Moira looking brighter. Ava, however, had to take her usual three calming breaths. She tried hard to hold on to some steadying memory. Surely her mother had once said, "You're always good in a crisis, Ava."

She had to cling to that.

Varo, promised to someone else, had got in over his head. So had she. It had all happened so fast. The effects had been mesmerising.

Ava moved to join Dev and Amelia's group. "You look ravishing, Ava!" Dev's tone spoke volumes of pride, while Amelia's expression showed her shared pleasure. "I have two beautiful women in my life."

Dev hugged Amelia to him. Plainly the two of them were enjoying themselves immensely. What she had to do now was not spoil things.

Plant a smile on your face.

A few moments later she felt without seeing that Varo had come to stand directly at her shoulder. He was greeted warmly by everyone, but it was Ava he had come for.

"I hope you realise, Ava, that as the captain of the winning team I am owed a dance by you. Several, in fact," he said, with his captivating smile.

She knew their guests were waiting for her response. And Mel, sharp as a tack, was watching her rather closely.

"Of course, Varo." She turned to him, her eyes ablaze in her face, brilliant as jewels.

Inside she might feel pale with shock, but outside she was all colour—the golden mane of hair, dazzling eyes, softly blushed cheeks, lovely deep pink mouth. She was determined now to play her part, her only wish to get through the night with grace. For all he hadn't been completely honest with her, Juan-Varo de Montalvo would never leave her memory, even when he disappeared to the other side of the world.

Varo took charge, as was his way. He clasped her hand in his, entwining his long fingers with hers, then led her away. Shaken, sobered, incredibly Ava felt *desire* course through her. Where had all this sensuality come from? These wildly extravagant reactions that touched every sensitive spot in her being and body? She had never experienced those feelings before. They had been drawn out of her by this man who had stolen her heart. There was just no fighting it. The connection was too strong.

Oh, God, she thought prayerfully. *Oh, God!* Her head was telling her what to do. Her body was ignoring the dictates of her mind. She had imagined him making love to her. Not a day had gone by when she hadn't fantasised about it. She felt possessed by him. Drawn like a moth to the flame. The huge problem was she couldn't seem to turn away from the flame, though she knew it could devour her.

"Wait," he murmured, steering her to the far corner of the loggia, just as she had known he would. In the light-dappled shadows he slowly turned her into his arms, his brilliant gaze questing. "What is troubling you, Ava?"

The sound of his name on her lips was like the softest swish of air. Yet pressure was expanding in her. *Be brave. Tell him.*

"Nothing." To her surprise her voice sounded normal. Or normal enough.

"Do you think I don't know you by now?"

The honeyed tenderness was almost her undoing. "But you don't *know* me, Varo. I don't know *you*."

He gave a soft laugh. "That is not quite correct." He took her into his arms as though the sole purpose for their coming to the far end of the terrace was to find a relatively quiet area to dance. "This is not the ideal moment to sort it out," he said humorously. "Too many people. Too many glowing lights. I cannot embrace you, or kiss your lovely mouth. I can only tell you I want you desperately." His full attention was focused on her. "You look incredibly beautiful." His arms tightened around her, guiding her in slow, sensual, graceful movements. *"Exquisito."*

What should she do? Their bodies were touching. She *couldn't* break away. Her muscles seemed to be locked. All she could do was stare into his dynamic dark face, wondering how she could live her life without him. It was quite frightening that she should think this way. But passion *was* frightening in its way.

He was wearing a white dinner jacket that served to emphasise his darkly tanned olive skin. It had to have been tailored for him because it fitted his wide shoulders like a glove. "Are you trying to woo me, Varo?" she asked, gripped by her undeniably erotic reaction. But this man *was* erotic. She had grasped that from the moment she had first laid eyes on him.

He was sensitive to her as well, because he had picked up on her mood. "Ava," he sighed over her head. "Ava. You want me to *win* you? Is that it?"

She placed a staying hand on his chest, feeling his heart beating strongly beneath the pristine white dress shirt. "You can't do that, of course," she said with a flare of spirit. "You have to return home soon."

"What *should* I do?" he countered swiftly, as though daring her. "Not for us coffee and conversation. Tell me, please, Ava."

It was a demand couched in exquisite gentleness. She struggled to find an answer but she was encased within his arms, her own heart beating as fast as a wild bird confined to a cage. "Is this all part of the adventure, Varo?"

The tenderness had alchemised to anger. Abruptly he pulled back, his handsome features tautening. "An adventure? What adventure?" A vertical line formed between his black brows. "I should stop your mouth with my own. Only I want to hear about these feelings that are plaguing you. You think me insincere? A social playboy?" He looked passionately affronted at the very idea. "I've fallen in love with you, Ava. Love is a force. The most powerful force on earth. I didn't expect any of this. I was not prepared. But we made an instant connection. You cannot deny it. Except, of course, as you say I don't really *know* you. However, you've allowed me to believe you are seriously affected as well. Or are you a witch?"

"I am *not* a witch," she said with adamance.

It was clear to her she had challenged his pride. He didn't like it. The deep dark emotions that were growing between them were as threatening as any storm. How long could they continue this fraught sensual dance before people began to notice?

Her face was turned up to his. She drew closer. "What about the woman you've left behind?" she accused. "The girlfriend? You told me your attentions were not engaged. Was that a lie?" Abruptly she recognised the fact she was madly jealous of the unknown young woman who no doubt would be stunningly beautiful. There would be strong approval from both families as well. That was the way it was done.

"Woman?" he rasped, as though she were completely stupid. "My God, is *that* it?"

"Of course that's *it*." Her supple body had gone rigid. The careless arrogance of his tone!

He wasn't going to let her go. He retained one of her hands as he stepped down a few steps into the garden and beyond to the radiant moonlight. He went first, compelling her to follow him into the scented darkness.

"Varo, what are you doing?" Her voice shook in alarm. "Where are we going?"

"Do not worry," he said. "Everything will be fine." He kept to the softly lit pathway, mindful of her evening shoes and her lovely long skirt.

She could smell gardenias. All kinds of beautiful blossoming flowers, native and exotic, and the scent of freshly clipped grass. "Varo!" she repeated breathlessly. If she had learned anything about herself it was that she couldn't resist him.

As they moved off the path into the deep shadows of the trees he caught her around the waist. "Who have you been speaking to?" he demanded. "Don't tell me. Sweet little Moira?"

She made no attempt to deny it. The brief conversation she had had with Moira had made her suffer. "You told her you had a special someone waiting for you at home." It was plain accusation.

"Maybe I was simply trying to get a message across?" he countered, his arm tightening around her as he drew her body, arched away from him, in close. "I'm not married. Who else to protect me but the woman I left behind?"

"Whose name is...?" The sad joke was on her!

"There *is* no one, Ava," he said very gently. Although

she knew he wouldn't forgive her if she continued to doubt
him. "Just part of my ploy so pretty little Moira wouldn't
waste her time," he explained. "If you raise your head a little
I can kiss your cheek. You have such beautiful skin. A perfect camellia comes into my mind. Sadly I can't kiss your
mouth as I want, because you can't return to the house *sin
carmín*. Your hawk-eyed cousin Karen would be so upset."

Why hadn't she figured it all out for herself? The idea of
Varo confiding in Moira had affected her so badly she had
made a quantum leap. "It was Karen who played a trick on
Moira," she confided abruptly. Her whole body was under
siege at his touch. "She told Moira you had picked her out
of the crowd."

He tilted her head back so he could run his mouth down
her cheek, over her delicate jawbone to the column of
her throat. "I would say your cousin is a woman full of
tricks." His mouth was warm against her skin. "*Peligrosa.*
Teacherous. Poor Moira was deliberately led astray. But one
wonders why…?"

"Karen wants to see what will happen, Varo."

"*Destino,*" he said, his hand sliding down over her breast
with unparallelled sensuality.

She shuddered, on the brink of surrender. "We have to
go back inside." It was imperative for her to take action before the pressure became too great.

"Soon. I need this badly." He sounded as if he was in
pain.

Ava bit her lip hard, so a moan wouldn't escape her. The
spell was at work again, holding them captive.

"Varo!" She forced her eyes open, her hand closing over
his at her breast.

"I know… I know…" A sigh was on his lips. He lifted
his head, his deep voice slightly slurred.

"I can't be sure," she told him in agitation, "but I think

there's someone moving beneath the trees." The trees were strung with countless tiny twinkling white lights, but there were dark spots.

Varo turned his head, his eyes trying to pierce the dappled dark. "A female puma, perhaps?" he mocked. "Why not acknowledge her?" There was more than a hint of derision in his tone. His resonant, fascinatingly accented voice lifted, carrying on the breeze. "We're over here, Karen," he called. "Feel free to join us. Ava is showing me the most wonderful night-blooming *cereus*."

He was quick witted—and he obviously knew the plant, native to Mexico. Because the cactus with its enormous breathtakingly beautiful creamy cups brimming with golden stamens was twined around a tree not a few feet away from them.

Silence.

"Perhaps I was mistaken?" Ava whispered, her whole body aquiver.

"Give it a minute." His voice was low in her ear. "Ah, the stalker shows herself!"

The ultra-thin figure of Karen, well camouflaged in her black gown, now appeared on the path, all but stomping towards them. "Oh, there you are!" she cried out in an artlessly playful voice that would have fooled no one. "I needed a break from all the noise. I expect you did too."

"What *is* this woman's problem?" Varo, still with his head bent, was murmuring in Ava's ear.

"I think she hates me." Karen was acting more like the enemy than her family.

"She will have to get to you through *me*." All of a sudden Varo sounded very cold and hard.

"I don't remember any night-blooming *cereus*," Karen was remarking caustically, looking dubiously around her.

"Ah, but Ava is far more knowledgeable." Varo spoke

with charming mockery. "You are standing midway between it and us."

"Oh, the cactus, you mean?" Karen's tone reduced the stunning beauty of the night-blooming *cereus* to that of a paper daisy.

"Breathtaking," Varo exclaimed, turning his raven head to Ava. "But I think it's high time for us to return to the party, don't you, Ava? *Muchas gracias* for showing me such beauty. Such a mystery why it only blooms at night."

CHAPTER SIX

THERE were not enough days in the following week. They flew by on the wings of mounting excitement. Nothing like a wedding to bring the thrill of joy. Although the great day had been organised down to the last little detail, there still remained things to do.

Amelia had been dropping weight with all the excitement; consequently her beautiful bridal gown needed adjustments.

Amelia's mother, Sarina, had been invited purely as a gesture, everyone knowing full well that Sarina was too busy living the good life in Tuscany.

Ava's husband, Luke Selwyn, had not been invited at all. He and Ava were divorcing, after all, and the split was far from amicable. Luke Selwyn made no bones about wanting Ava back, although he had told Ava many times he wasn't happy with her. There had always been something she wasn't getting quite right. But he *wanted* her. No mistaking that. And she *was* the Langdon heiress.

The homestead, with its twelve bedrooms extended from the original ten, all fitted with an *en suite* bathroom, was full up. So too was the accommodation at the men's quarters, the dormitories, and all the various bungalows—including the one-teacher schoolhouse—that sat like satellites around the main compound.

People streamed through the house, carrying all sorts of boxes for all purposes. A huge consignment of glorious flowers had been flown in from Sydney, along with a renowned floral designer and his team. Top musicians had arrived. Food and drink and a team of caterers were to be flown in first thing Saturday morning.

The ceremony, in the lovely tranquillity of the garden, was to take place at four p.m., after the heat of the day had abated. Vows would be exchanged beneath an eighteenth-century gazebo with carved stone pillars and a delicate white cupola. Great urns nearby had been filled with white cymbidium orchids that had been flown in from Thailand. No expense had been spared. This was a once-in-a-lifetime event—a marriage that was destined to endure.

Dev's best man and his two grooms had arrived in the best man's private Cessna. Amelia's other bridesmaids arrived on Friday. A rehearsal was to take place in the late afternoon.

The reception was to be held in the Great Hall, a large multi-purpose building separate from the house. A celebration barbecue had been organised for Kooraki's staff. It was scheduled to begin at the same time as the main reception. This was a splendid occasion, affecting everyone on the station.

Amelia had bypassed the traditional structured duchesse satin style for a much lighter look perfect for a hot early summer's afternoon. The bride and her three bridesmaids were to wear the same exquisitely hand embroidered chiffon over full-length silk slips. Amelia had chosen for her bridesmaids the soft colours of one of her favourite flowers, the hydrangea. Amelia's own gown, ivory-white, was lightly embroidered with tiny pearls and sparkling beads to within some six or seven inches from the hem, where the embroidery burst into large silver leaves that gleamed like a work of art.

Ava was to wear not the blue of the hydrangea but another colour that suited her beautifully: an exquisite mauve. The other bridesmaids, Lisa and Ashleigh, would be wearing hydrangea-blue and pink. Slender arms were to be left bare. Instead of a veil Amelia would be wearing a floral diadem to encircle her dark head. So too would her bridesmaids. All would wear their long hair loose and flowing. Each bridesmaid's heart-shaped posy would feature one of the flowers in the bride's white bouquet, whether rose, peony, butterfly orchid, hydrangea or lily.

It had been a close collaboration, with input from each bridesmaid as to colours and styles. It was a great good fortune all were tall and slim with long flowing hair. Amelia did not want a *grand* wedding, as such. She wanted a lovely summer's day fantasy. A romantic wedding above all.

Amelia's room was crowded with her bridesmaids, the dresser and hairdresser and Elizabeth, Dev and Ava's mother. Even Karen had found her way in, standing near the open French doors, studying them all with a strange expression—never pleasure or excitement—on her tight-skinned face. She had chosen to wear a black and white outfit, extremely smart, but Ava thought it would have been nicer had she worn a colour.

The instant before Ava stepped into the corridor after the others Karen caught her arm. "Surely you're thinking of someone outside yourself today?" she asked in a steely voice.

Ava turned around, resolving to keep her temper. "Please don't upset me, Karen. It would be entirely the wrong day. What *is* your problem with me, anyway? You've always had one."

"I've had a purpose," said Karen, "to look out for you. And I place a lot of importance on marriage vows." She lowered her voice as Amelia looked back over her shoulder to check on them.

"Wait until *you* get there, Karen," Ava said. "How old are you now?"

Karen's expression became slightly pinched. "I've had any number of offers, Ava. I'm taking my time. I don't intend to make a mistake, like you. And you *are* making a mistake. Luke loves you. He wants you back. Hard to understand why, when you've treated him so badly."

The unfairness of it all!

Ava shook her cousin's hand off just as Amelia moved back to them, a slight frown on her beautiful face.

"Tell me you're not trying to upset Ava?" She stepped right up to Karen, so Karen had to fall back a step or two.

Just like in their schooldays, Ava thought. Mel stepping in to protect her.

"Mel, everything's okay," she said, ever the peacemaker.

But Mel, of Italian descent, had a volcanic temper when aroused.

"Let's say I was trying to talk sense to Ava." Karen adopted a self-righteous pose. "I happen to care about her. She *is* my cousin. I care about Luke too. He's suffering."

"Suffering?" Mel exploded. "Are you serious? Luke Selwyn is your classic narcissist. And a womaniser. As if you didn't know. If you like him so much, Karen, he'll be available in the not so distant future. Look him up. Offer comfort. But, for now, keep out of Ava's affairs. She is *not* your concern. And another thing! How dare you cause upset on *my* wedding day?" Mel's delicate nostrils flared. "Honestly, Karen, you're so stupid you don't even know you're stupid. Here's a word of warning from the bride: *behave.*"

Karen visibly deflated. Amelia had always had that effect on her—that was why she hated her. She gave a strangled laugh. "I can assure you, Amelia, I'll do the best I can."

"Be sure you do," said Amelia with a sharp nod.

"You look wonderful, by the way."

"Thank you so much, Karen," Mel said ironically. "Come along, Ava. This is one bride who isn't going to be late for her wedding."

At four o'clock, in a haze of emotion, the wedding ceremony took place. Bride and groom exchanged vows beneath the shelter of the white wrought-iron lace of a cupola decorated with white flowers and satin ribbons. Amelia stood in her exquisite bridal gown, sewn all over with sparkling crystals, staring up into her beloved Dev's eyes.

It was an ageless ritual but incredibly moving. Ava, ethereal in her mauve bridesmaid's gown, bowed her blonde diadem-encircled head in prayer, the inevitable tears rising to her eyes.

God bless and protect you all the days of your lives. God grant you beautiful children to love and raise to the highest possible level of happiness, confidence and morality.

Dev and Amelia were strong people. They had endured years of conflict—as had she. Only she had been the one who had been openly frightened of her grandfather but desperately anxious to win his approval. Her father had had the same experience, but those days were gone. Life had become more complicated, but in a way very much simpler. They were all working towards the same goal: personal fulfilment within a secure family environment. Dev had his adored wife. She had a sister. Their parents, reunited, had their eyes set on the future. And, needless to say—grandchildren to love and very likely spoil.

The ceremony over, the newly married couple yielded

completely to the bridal kiss. Emotion spread across the garden area. Women guests happily dabbed tears from their eyes, irresistibly reminded of *their* wedding day.

"The happiest day!" Elizabeth Langdon, looking lovely in a short blue silk shift with a matching lace jacket and a filmy blue picture hat whispered to her daughter, "Your perfect day is yet to come, my darling."

Hope that had glimmered, brightened, strengthened by Ava's wildly blossoming emotions, turned as insubstantial as gauze.

In the reception hall white-linen-draped buffet tables were laden with a succulent gastronomic feast: hams, turkeys, chicken dishes—hot and cold—roast duck and lamb, all manner of scrumptious seafood, whole Tasmanian salmons—cold and smoked—reef fish, lobsters, prawns, sea scallops, mussels and oysters, salads galore...

Good-looking young waiters were almost pirouetting, pouring champagne, white wine, red, and the popular rosé. There was also a well-stocked bar for anything stronger, and gallons of icy cold fruit juices and soft drinks.

There was a separate table groaning under the weight of desserts: apricot, peach, banana, mango, berries, citrus cakes and tarts, coconut cakes, and the all-time favourite chocolate desserts. No one would go away feeling hungry. This was a *serious* banquet the like of which was seldom seen.

From the upstairs gallery in the homestead Amelia, now mistress of Kooraki, threw her exquisite grandiflora bouquet: white roses, luxurious white peonies with the faintest flush of pink, gardenia *"magnifica,"* a perfect velvety white, a single large head of white hydrangea and a small cluster of butterfly orchids. She threw it directly towards her chief bridesmaid. Such was her accuracy, Ava had no option but to catch it.

Karen, who was behind Ava, leaned forward to whisper, "I seem to remember you've *already* been given in wedlock."

Nothing, it seemed, could stop Karen. It was a wonder she didn't shout it from the top of her lungs. She wasn't a woman of great subtlety. Even so, Ava found it hard not to remember that fact too. She had ignored all good advice. For once she had made her own decision. Well, it had cost her.

But her grandfather had left her financially set for life. Probably he had never trusted her to determine her own future. Even now she had fallen madly in love with a man who would soon return to his own country, his own life. She had thrown herself wide open to him. They couldn't go backwards. They could only go forward. Varo was only seeing what he wanted to see. Varo wanted her. She knew that. Fate had put her in his path. But Varo had other people to think of. His family in Argentina. They would have important concerns and plans for their only son. In her wildest dreams she didn't think they would accept a divorced woman. Their son could have *anyone*! Any beautiful young woman in their circle. Not a woman from another place. One who couldn't even speak Spanish.

Had Varo's American mother been fluent in Spanish when she'd run off with her Argentine husband? In all likelihood she hadn't been, but neither of them had cared.

By seven o'clock the newlyweds had left to fly to Sydney. The following morning they would board a fight to Singapore, staying at Raffles for a few days before heading off for London, their first European port of all.

This was the signal for the party to step up a gear. No

one wanted the wonderful day to end. It was all so exciting, with everyone so friendly. The older guests retired to
the house for long in-depth conversations; the under forties
were dead set on having a good time.

There was a great deal of laughter, flirting and, it had to
be said, drinking. And dancing to a great band that became
more and more high-powered as the night went on was on
everyone's agenda. The band members were enjoying themselves every bit as much as the guests. They'd been well
fed, and they hadn't gone short on liquid refreshments. No
one was counting.

Varo pushed his chair back towards the shelter of a lush
golden cane in a splendid blue and white Chinese jardinière.
He had been enjoying more than his fair share of female
attention, and now he was thankful to be on his own for the
moment—free to watch Ava make her way down the staircase with her signature flowing grace, a romantic fantasy in
her lovely softest mauve dress. She had removed the silver
diadem she had worn around her head for the ceremony. It
had suited her perfectly, enhancing the ethereal look. He
had loved the idea of the diadem for a headdress. It had
been set here and there along its length with tiny real roses
nestled into little sprays of sparkling crystals.

Dev had given each bridesmaid a necklace to match her
gown. Varo imagined they would treasure it: hand-made
pendants featuring large diamond-set gemstones hanging
from delicate white gold chains. Ava's gemstone was an
amethyst, Lisa's a pink sapphire, Ashleigh's a blue topaz.
They had all looked beautiful, with their long flowing hair
and filmy summer dresses. He had danced several times
with both Lisa and Ashleigh. Now he was waiting for Ava,
who was proving as elusive as a woodland nymph.

As he looked towards the staircase he felt a sudden chill

that had him turning in his chair. It couldn't be. But it was. Cousin Karen had appeared again.

"Hi, there!"

She pulled up a chair close to him, crossing her long legs. She was looking very elegant in her black and white gown, but he found himself feeling astonishingly hostile to her. This rarely happened to him—especially with a woman. But there it was!

"Well, that went off extremely well, didn't it?" Karen had prepared a big smile, and was speaking in an enthusiastic kind of voice that didn't fool him one bit. "Slightly odd, Amelia throwing her bouquet to Ava," she slid in, her dark eyes hooded.

"You expected Amelia to throw it to *you*?" he asked suavely.

"No, no!" she protested laughingly. "Lord knows *I'm* in no hurry to marry. I simply meant Ava is already married. Divorce may be streamlined here in Australia—one year and one day of separation. Why the extra day?" she trilled. "But it has to *be* that before an application can be filed in the court. A hearing date can take a couple of months. You may not know this, but that separation date hasn't yet been reached."

"Why are you telling me this?" Varo asked, successfully staring her down. He really wanted to get away from this woman as he would want to get away from a snake.

She made a sound like a strangled giggle. "Go figure! I thought you and Ava were on the verge of having an affair?"

He recognised malevolence when he encountered it. "You think this, do you? Or do you fear it? And would it be *your* business either way?" His voice he kept low, but his black eyes took on a brilliant diamond-like glitter.

Karen could see he was angry. He really was a magnificent man. "Well, I've made it my business because I care about Ava, Varo," she insisted—not for the first time. "And Luke. As I've told you, he worships her."

"Apparently she missed that," he said, with heavy irony.

"Oh, no!" Karen shook her shiny dark bob that was groomed to racehorse perfection. "It was apparent to everyone who knew them or met them. Luke adores her. She's his perfect princess."

"So it's all Ava's fault? Is that it?"

Karen sighed, holding up one of her manicured hands to avoid his penetrating eyes. "Fault? No, I never said fault. But Ava is a fragile creature. She always has been."

"Perhaps she needs a *real* man and not your Luke?" Varo suggested smoothly. He rose to his impressive six-three, a stunningly handsome man, and stared down at Ava's poisonous cousin. "Would it clarify anything in your mind if I said you cannot hide your jealousy of Ava? I suspect it has always been there. She's so beautiful, and I have noted she takes into account *everyone's* feelings. I would say before her own."

Karen appeared genuinely shocked by his action. She too rose to her feet, colour flagging her high cheekbones. "It's much too soon for you to make an assessment, Varo. I'm only trying to prevent a huge mistake."

"And you would be desolate if your little plan came awry?" he challenged. "I think this is all a deliberate attempt at sabotage, Ms Devereaux. Now, if you will excuse me, I plan to dance with Ava."

Karen shook her head sadly. "My conscience is clear. I've done my level best."

"I would say you have. Only it's your motivation that is being questioned. Rest assured, Ms Devereaux, we can handle this ourselves."

Karen blushed and turned away, a white-hot fury moving through her. She would get even with Ava if it was the last thing she did. She was already going along that road, blind to anything else. She didn't really know or understand *why*, but she had always wanted to rob her cousin in some way. She especially wanted to rob her of any chance she might have with the arrogant, supremely macho Argentine. To think she had half fancied him too! He had certainly got her adrenaline going for a while. Now she hated him. Few men intimidated her. Juan-Varo de Montalvo did.

Varo drained a vodka before he went in search of the elusive Ava, who had disappeared. Eventually he found her out on the terrace, dancing with one of the polo-players, a long-time family friend and, as he correctly guessed, a long-time admirer of Ava.

He tapped the polo-player's shoulder, his name having sprung to mind. "May I cut in, Jeff?" he asked lightly. "Ava has promised me my quota of dances."

Jeff didn't look the least put out. "You're saying I've had mine?" He laughed, lingeringly releasing Ava. "Indeed, I have."

"Muchas gracias!" Varo smiled at the other man, who smiled back. Varo then took Ava very smoothly into his arms, their feet immediately fitting the soft, slow romantic beat. "You see me. You disappear again," he chided gently.

She tilted her face to him, caught up in the same physical exhilaration, the sense of *belonging*. "I saw Karen pull up a chair beside you. I didn't like to interrupt."

He gave an exaggerated groan. "Please *do* if there is ever a next time."

His arresting face was all high cheekbones, striking planes and angles in the shadowy golden light. "What was she saying this time?" she asked.

His voice dropped to a low, confiding whisper. "You don't want to know." He gathered her in close, feeling his hunger for her tighten into the now familiar near-painful knots of tension. He only had so much strength to resist such magical allure.

"Possibly what Karen should do is train to become a private investigator," Ava said thoughtfully.

"I promise you she'd be good at it." He laughed.

"So what *did* she say?" Ava persisted, very glad her cousin was going home the following day.

"Same old thing." Varo shrugged. "Your husband wants you back." He hesitated a moment, then said, "Could you tell me how long it is since you've been separated from him?"

They seemed to be dancing alone. Other couples had drifted away. "Ah, now, I'm ninety-nine point nine percent sure Karen told you."

His tone was taut. "I don't listen to Karen. I listen to *you*."

"Why talk about it on a day like today?" She sighed, swaying like a feather in his arms.

"Why refuse when it is something that is important to me?" he countered, steering her into the light so he could capture her exact expression.

Ava realised his intention. "Luke and I are two months short of the mandatory separation time, Varo," she said. "Which is exactly as Karen must have told you: one year and one day. The day after my solicitor will file my application in the court. Luke no longer has a hold on me, Varo. My marriage is over."

"You think the court will look favourably on your application for divorce?" They had stopped dancing, but he was holding her in place.

"Why not?" she fired, her beautiful eyes ablaze. "My solicitor—he's a top man—has assured me it will."

"Your husband may throw difficulties in your way," Varo said. She felt so soft, so silken, so fluid in his arms she might have been naked beneath her exquisite sheer dress. "Perhaps you will be told to provide more information?"

The music had stopped. Now it started up again. Of all things, the famous Bolero. It was being played by the band with a compulsive up beat and a strong tango rhythm. Instinctively their interlocked bodies reacted. Along the length of the terrace other couples devoted themselves to their own form of the tango, while trying to keep within the spirit of the dance. Certainly the embrace was high on their list, with strong body connections, heads and faces touching.

"I know I have to be careful," Ava said, her voice unsteady. "I think we both know Karen will be reporting to Luke the minute she gets back home. If she hasn't done so already. I have come to the sad conclusion there's nothing my cousin wouldn't do to hurt me."

His body was finding it impossible not to move into the dance he knew so intimately. What woman could he desire more than Ava? When he was with her he felt somehow complete.

"When does she leave?" he asked rather curtly beneath his breath.

"Midday tomorrow."

He held her in a formal open embrace, gauging her knowledge of the dance. She followed him in total communication, arching her upper body away in the "ballroom" style of tango she would have been taught. She would know the famous dance had originated in Buenos Aires, but she didn't as yet know the striking difference between the Argentine tango and the positions and steps she had learned.

Only he would show her...

Ava felt rapt, carried along by sensation and responding perfectly to his signals. "You're such a beautiful dancer, Varo," she breathed, in a trance of pleasure.

"So are you. But your style is a little…formal. Let me show you." He moved her in close. Her breasts were against his chest, but there was a space between their hips. "Relax now. Relax totally," he said hypnotically. "Follow where I lead. Argentine tango continually changes. It is very improvisational. Emotion is extremely important. We have that, do we not?"

She felt desperately moved by his words. Did he *mean* them? Or was he giving way to infatuation? She was still so unsure of herself. Karen's planned intervention hadn't helped. They were dancing around the perimeter of the broad spacious terrace. The rhythm in his body, the musicality, seemed sublime. She had never known anything approaching it. It lifted her own dance skills, which she had been told many times were exceptional. But not like *this*. This was a communion of bodies…of souls…

No one cut across them. Everyone was now sticking to their own "lane", casting frequent glances at Varo and Ava and what they were doing. It might have been a master class, with a group of advanced students following the master's lead.

After a while—though Ava was scarcely aware of it, so caught up was she in the dance—the other couples cleared the terrace until it resembled a stage. The tango was the most passionate, the most exciting dance of them all. And here it was being so beautifully, so thrillingly performed on this wondrous day of days.

The wave upon wave of applause was sincere. Couples surrounded them, clapping and chanting, *"Bravo!"*

"That was the best example of the tango I've ever seen," exclaimed a flushed-faced Moira O'Farrell—no mean dancer herself. "I had no idea you were such a terrific dancer, Ava. So *sexy*!"

"This is the day to kick over the traces," her partner supplied.

In fact Ava had surprised them all—almost transfigured from the lovely, serene Ava they knew. She had packed so much *passion* into the famous dance it had been startling to those who knew her. Of course the Argentine was a past master. And the right partner was of tremendous importance. But neither had in any way been consciously showing off. It had passed way beyond that. It had appeared more like one glorious, even blatant, seduction.

The party broke up about three o'clock. The band had ceased playing an hour before that. Time to catch a few hours' sleep before the lavish brunch that was being served from eight o'clock onwards.

All the older guests had long since turned in. Finally the last stragglers went in search of their accommodation. Ava felt it her duty to remain at the party until the very end. Her mother and father had gone off on the crest of a wave, some time before one a.m., declaring themselves thrilled everything had gone so well.

"You don't see a lot of Karen, do you, darling?" her mother had asked, after kissing her goodnight.

"Not really." Ava had kept her smile.

"Good. I never liked that girl. She's rather unpleasant. For once I agree with your late grandfather. He never liked her either. You've got your own life, darling. She has hers. Hate to say it, but I don't trust her." Elizabeth's fine eyes had met those of her daughter's. "Be on your guard," she'd warned.

Ava went around the ground floor turning off all the main lights but leaving on a few lamps. There was no one around now. Oddly enough she didn't feel in the least tired.

She felt wired. It was a kind of refined torture—wanting someone desperately, having to keep oneself apart.

Varo had raised the point of the period of separation. Her application was a few months off being filed. She had an enemy in the house. In her cousin. Luke, for whatever reason, did seem intent on getting her back. Control was natural to men. Maybe even the *best* of men. She could pay a heavy price for allowing herself to have become so involved with Varo.

God, it's worth it!

She took the rear staircase to the upper floor, moving cautiously so as not to make any noise. Now, why did she do that? Was she deliberately playing with fire? Was she out of control? She could see Varo had not gone to bed, although they had said their formal goodnights thirty minutes ago. His bedroom was still illuminated. A shaft of light was raying under the door. She stood in the corridor, staring down the length of it. Wall sconces remained on, shedding a soft light.

All was silence. All was utterly still. The house slept.

She moved on soundless feet towards Varo's door, as if it was some forbidden rite. Her long chiffon skirt softly swished around her ankles. Her heart was beating in a frantic, unnatural way. She tossed her long hair over her shoulder, although golden strands clung to her heated cheeks.

What are you doing?

Her inner voice spoke up so sharply she backed away from the door, feeling a surge of panic.

You're not divorced from Luke yet.

Even so, she stood glued to the spot.

If I'm punished, I deserve it.

Astonishingly, as if he had a super sixth sense, Varo's door came open and his strong arm drew her swiftly inside as if she were a puppet on a string. Tingles started up all over her body...exquisite...probing. She began to flush from head to toe, as though molten liquid was being poured into her. She felt radiant, intoxicated, fearful.

"Varo, what are you doing?" Even her voice sounded afraid.

"Waiting for you. What else?" His dark eyes glittered as they rested on her. Her long blonde hair floated sinuously around her lovely camellia-skinned face, framing it. He could clearly see the pulse beating in the hollow at the base of her neck. That excited him. Her sparkling eyes were huge. Such emotion, such appeal was in them, it only served to inflame his passion.

"Dear Lord," she whispered. "This is *madness!*"

Madness. The word seemed to echo around the room, bouncing gently off the walls.

"Far better than doing nothing," he returned tautly, drawing her into his warm, close embrace. "Let me tell you about my mother and father when they were young. They surrendered to madness too—only they called it *love.*"

Words of protest kept coming and going inside her head, but she didn't utter a one. She knew full well she was doing something dangerous. She knew she should be careful. But she wasn't a thinking woman in his arms. She lifted her face to him like a flower to the sun in the sky for its blessing. Tenderly he began to trace the contours of her mouth with a padded finger.

The sensation that poured into her made her shudder. She took his finger into her mouth, her tongue caressing it.

"Don't be afraid," he said.

"Varo, I am. Technically I'm still married." Her voice was strained, full of intensity.

His answer was a mix of hard authority and deep emotion. "It's not you and Luke any more. It's you and me."

"But *how*? You will go away soon. You could forget all

about me. You might say you'll call me, e-mail me—God knows I'd spend my time checking—but once you get home things will be different. Family affairs will keep you very busy. You said you and your father had big plans." She knew she might be left with nothing but a broken heart.

Except he said, very simply, "We wait a while."

Was she to agree to that? Why could she not find her voice? Of course she *had* to wait. Even without Luke's throwing up difficulties, and if her application was successful, the decree nisi would only become final one month and one day from the date of the divorce order. She still didn't know how soon her application would come before the court. What she did know was that she and Varo had reached the point of no return. She had confirmed that by hovering outside his door. He with his finely tuned sensibilities had known she would come to him. He had been waiting as though it were her decision.

Wasn't that your objective? her inner voice questioned sharply.

Yearning rose in her body as his mouth came down across her hair, her forehead, her nose, her cheek. She tipped her head back so he could kiss her throat, before he came back to settle on her receptive open mouth. No feigning of emotion with Varo. No pretence. No mechanical movements. No sense of a deep inner loneliness, lying beneath a man unfulfilled. Varo had lit up every last little part of her with passion. Pure passion. How often did one meet a man with whom one was in perfect accord?

She stood quietly while he removed her beautiful glimmering dress with extreme care, leaving her body covered by the mauve silk slip. Her light, slender limbs had turned heavy, as if she wanted to lie down. He must have known, because he lifted her high in his arms before placing her very gently on the turned-back bed.

"I would not harm you for the world, Ava," he murmured. His lustrous eyes burned. "I only want to love you a little. Give you pleasure. I will wait for you. For the right time. Have no fear. You have only to tell me to stop if you fear I go too far. I want making love to you to be so *natural*." His eyes on her were very brilliant, very tender.

Her whole body was drowning in sensation. She closed her eyes, feeling the heat of her sex but knowing this time was not to be their ultimate encounter. There were demands to be met. "Everything is natural with you," she whispered, as he kissed her inner wrist with its white translucence and faint tracery of blue veins.

"As it should be," he said softly, bending his head to kiss her gently, so gently, cupping her face with his hands.

All he knew was his desire, but he had made a vow not to seduce her into giving herself. The depth of feeling he had for her, the tenderness, the sense of protectiveness, was as potent as it was astounding. He broke contact with her mouth, controlling the fever. His eyes followed his hands. He drew them, imperceptibly trembling, down over the length of her, the indentation of her narrow waist, her hips, her thighs, her long slender legs. He didn't realise it but he was murmuring in Spanish.

"You are a revelation to me."

Such beauty!

He was inhaling the fragrance that rose from her body, his sex hardening, but that was something he could not control. Lovemaking without penetration could be an enormous stress on a man's body, but the lovemaking still retained many elements of rapture.

Convulsively Ava moved, so he could lie more comfortably beside her on the bed. These were Varo's hands on her, kissing, stroking through the silk of the light bra and wisteria-coloured silk slip that covered her. Oddly, it seemed incredibly erotic. At some point she felt the cool breeze hit her naked breasts. Her senses were flooded with the warmth and the clean male scent of him. Lovemaking with Varo was an extraordinary bewitching ritual. She could hear little whimpering sounds. They were issuing from her own lips. All there was was her desire for him; his desire for her. She kept her eyes tightly closed, lost in a world of exquisite sensation.

At one point she found herself gripping his strong naked back in an effusion of heat and light, desperate to give him as much pleasure as he was giving her. He had thrown off his shirt long ago. They were both turning and twist-ing, bodies interlocking, totally absorbed the one in the other, their bodies imploring, wanting consummation. Varo wanted to know the whole of her, her glorious white flesh. She was allowing it. He was finding it near impossible to hold off the brilliant, overpowering rush of blind sex. Her beautiful body had already dissolved beneath his hands. He knew, like him, she could barely withstand the flood of sensation.

His steely resolve was under threat. She was his. Those inciting little exhalations! They were like a torch held against his skin.

With a deep groan, his handsome face near tortured, he began to breathe deeply, mustering control. Then he very gently began to ease her bra and her silk slip back onto her delicate white shoulders, kissing one and then the other.

"Ava, I have to stop," he muttered.

She opened her jewelled eyes to him. "I know." She put up a caressing hand to stroke his handsome chiselled face, moving her hand to clasp his nape, damp from his rising temperature. Their lovemaking, however curtailed, had been agony and ecstasy both. A rapture too extravagant to describe. She had to marvel, and then bless Varo's capacity for control. She had been lost, adrift in a sea of sensation.

He fell back on the bed beside her, staring up at the orante plaster rose in the ceiling. "I knew it would be you," he murmured, almost to himself. "I knew it in that very first moment."

"As did I." Ava's response came from the depths of her heart.

That was the great mystery of it all. Destiny at work. Only the heart, once given, could never be recalled.

Ava knew beyond all question that she had given hers.

CHAPTER SEVEN

THE first thing Luke Selwyn did when he got up that morning, after yet another anger-racked night, was check his e-mail. He was hoping for some communication from Karen. Karen was a good sort—a loyal pal. He should have married someone like Karen, only she was totally lacking in sex appeal. *That* his poor Ava had in abundance. The joke was she didn't know it.

He was absolutely furious—his parents were too—that they hadn't been invited to Langdon's wedding to *that woman's* daughter. He would always think of Amelia as that. The irony of it all. She was now mistress of Kooraki, wife to the man in control of the Langdon fortunes. Amelia—who had looked at him with blazing contempt.

Bitch!

Karen hated her too. There were five messages from her in his in-box. Only *one* was he interested in. He opened that message first, read the contents—his wife was having a great time, was she?—then opened the attachment, wondering what it would contain.

What he saw made him sit down joltingly hard at his desk. How dared she? *How dared she?* A peculiar fury was racing through him. He had always had the upper hand with Ava, physically and psychologically. She had never rebelled, never protested—except at anything a bit adventurous he had wanted in the bedroom. Such a prude!

Her first and only deliberate act of rebellion had been in defying that tyrannical old bastard of a grandfather to marry *him*. Her second major rebellion had been in leaving him. Her betrayal would have left him desolated—only he knew he could force her back, and when he did he'd make her pay. No one was going to ditch him. Not even the heiress Ava Langdon-Selwyn. Her shocking lack of allegiance would cost her. He couldn't wait.

He clenched his fists in his lap, biting down involuntarily on his tongue. He tasted blood in his mouth. The attachment showed three shots of his wife dancing with some South American gigolo. As flamboyantly handsome as any matinee idol and a polo-player of all things. He couldn't believe their body language. *His* Ava! She looked like a member of some professional dance troupe, strutting her stuff. The final shot had him swearing aloud. The dance was a tango. Anyone would know that. And there was his precious frigid Ava, holding a pose that should never be. This was his *wife*, dammit! The fact that Ava could act in this abandoned way made him dizzy with rage. She wasn't going to be allowed to make a fool of him. No way!

The insufferably arrogant Langdon was away on his honeymoon with his equally arrogant wife. He hoped they had a miserable time of it. Terrible weather. Food poisoning. Lost luggage. Anything to spoil their dream time. He hated his brother-in-law with a passion. Now he hated his own wife. But he still wanted her. Oh, yes, he wanted her. He enjoyed their life together. He enjoyed controlling her. Only she had hurt him. So it was only fitting he would hurt her. The gigolo wouldn't present a problem, even if he did manage to stay on a while after Ava's parents returned home. He could easily find out when the Langdons were back in town. Arranging a charter flight to Kooraki would be easy enough.

Perhaps he ought to adopt the grieving-husband role? Enlist the gigolo's sympathies if he were still there? He was the husband, after all. It might not be far off but the application for divorce had not been filed. There was time for reconciliation. Ava knew her duty. Her duty was to him. The gigolo would see that. It wasn't as though he was after commitment. His life was in Argentina. Ava would never go there. The very thought of being away from her family would alarm her. A real cream puff was Ava.

Nevertheless, the shock of what he had seen had him still sitting in his chair a good twenty minutes later, staring all the while at a silver-framed photograph of his beautiful wife. It had pride of place on his desk. He still had her photograph on his desk at the office too. He knew Ava so well he took cold comfort in the fact she was extremely cautious by nature. No way would she have sex with a stranger. God, no! Ava had dozens of ardent admirers, who would give anything to spend a stolen hour with her. But Ava had never been unfaithful, was totally loyal. He trusted her completely. He'd had other women, of course. But that was different. Men were different. Men had different needs.

Her parents stayed on for a few days, at peace with one another and clearly enjoying themselves. They had taken a great liking to Varo, drawing closer to him every day. Clearly he was an exceptional young man who loved his family, his extended family, his country.

"Varo has a wonderful blend of sense and sensibility," Elizabeth remarked to her daughter. "It has such power to attract."

Elizabeth and Erik had derived great enjoyment from Varo's sense of humour, and his fascinating tales of Argentina and his family life there. He had invited them to stay at Estancia de Villaflores whenever they visited South America, which he hoped would be soon. The invitation had been issued with such genuine warmth both felt they might indeed take him up on it. Varo had assured them most charmingly that the *estancia* had as many guest rooms as Kooraki. His parents loved entertaining.

On the morning Ava's parents were to return home, Elizabeth sought a few private words with her daughter.

"You're in love with him, aren't you?" Elizabeth asked calmly and without preamble. She was half reclining on the chaise in Ava's bedroom, looking across at her daughter, who was sitting very quietly on the carved chest at the end of her bed.

Ava took a deep breath. She'd known this was coming. Her eyes met those of her mother. "I thought I was being *friendly*," she said, with a wry smile.

Elizabeth couldn't help laughing. "My darling, I'm a woman. I'm your mother. I understand perfectly why you're in love with him. What woman wouldn't be? He has *everything*." Elizabeth made an expansive little gesture. "He's everything Luke isn't."

Ava looked out at the gently swaying palms. "Of course he is. Do you think he loves me?"

Elizabeth smiled. "I may not have personally experienced the legendary *coup de foudre*, but I would say you two have. Your father agrees. He's very happy about it. The more the two of you attempt to play down your feelings, the more intense they appear. Have you slept with him?"

Ava felt her hot blush. *"Mum!"*

"Sorry, darling," Elizabeth apologised. "Only, you have

the radiance of a woman who is not only in love but is loved. What is Varo saying about the future?" she questioned with a slight frown. "He has deep ties to his family. He loves his own country."

Ava sighed. "I know that, Mum. All he says is, 'We wait a while.'"

"Implying?"

"I don't ask." Ava's shrug was a shade helpless. "I can't believe what is happening to me, Mum. I need a little time for the miracle to sink in. I never thought I could ever feel like this. I even thought I had a cool heart, if not cold. No, don't scoff. Luke was forever driving that point home. Maybe I can't believe it could ever work out for Varo and me. I can't even believe the divorce will proceed without incident. Luke is storing up trouble. He's like that. He'll throw anything he can in the way of holding up proceedings."

"So who's to talk?" Elizabeth asked derisively. "We're a thousand miles from anywhere. Luke knows nothing. Although I realise that dreadful girl Karen has always been his informant. Are you sure she's not keen on him herself?"

Ava shook her head. "Luke doesn't find Karen attractive. In fact he's said many an unkind thing about her. Her figure, in particular. How thin she is. He uses her, that's all."

"She could tell him about your famous dance…" Elizabeth said reflectively.

"Heard about it, did you?" Ava asked. Her parents had gone to bed before then.

"Certainly did." Elizabeth laughed. "You've always been a lovely dancer, but from all accounts you excelled yourself."

Ava's eyes were glitter-bright. "You know perfectly well how a wonderful partner can raise your performance. The tango is in Varo's blood."

"I bet!" Elizabeth laughed again. "The two of you must promise a repeat performance some time." Reluctantly she rose. "The wedding was simply marvellous. And it was lovely to hear from Dev and Amelia and know they're so blissfully happy." And now it seemed to Elizabeth her beloved daughter might have found the man of her dreams. "When is Varo going home?" she asked as they walked to the door. "He's come a long way. He will want to see lots more. The Red Centre was mentioned. Uluru and Kata Tjuta. He's so enjoying himself."

"I'm not pressing him for an answer," Ava said. "Rather the reverse."

She didn't say such thoughts and accompanying fears were never far from her mind. What would Varo's inevitable return to Argentina do to their relationship, for one? That was the burning question. She had to accept conflicts would arise. Could she give up her homeland for Varo? Could she leave the people she loved? She couldn't see that far into the future. Really, it all came down to Varo. If Varo loved her, all would be well.

Elizabeth put her arm around her daughter, hugging her close. "I want you to be happy, Ava. I pray for you to be happy. You're a lovely woman—inside and out. A wonderful loving daughter. Don't let Luke Selwyn intimidate you. I know it was the case in the past, his manipulation, though you never said anything. Dev and Amelia will be back home by the separation date—the year and the day. You have me and your father. We will be with you. Staying with a loveless marriage would be like being in a prison. The divorce *will* go through, my darling. You've a top lawyer. You're going to come out of this."

"One day, Mum," Ava said, her lovely smile a touch on the melancholy side.

* * *

She had to go in search of Varo. They had seen her parents off, and had a leisurely lunch over which they'd discussed where they would go on the station that afternoon.

It was a strange time for Ava, a euphoric time. She had the feeling the whole universe had changed. Simultaneously she wouldn't be shocked if it reverted to what it had been. Love affairs always started out with high hopes. She had even had hopes for herself and Luke, but never euphoria. Euphoria was like riding an ocean wave.

She thought she might take Varo out to see Malyah Man. The extraordinary rock formation was semi-sacred to the aboriginals on the station. It was a truly amazing spectacle, some eight feet tall, and resembled an aboriginal head atop a fiery limestone column rather like a Henry Moore sculpture or the Easter Island figures. Malyah Man stood alone in the remoteness, quite a distance beyond where they had so far gone.

She had been in awe of the rock all her life. There was something daunting about it, but it was certainly a sight worth seeing. Like all the rock formations on the station it changed colour from dawn to dusk. At midday it was a furnace-red that quickly lost intensity and became a reddish brown. By the end of the day it glowed a deep purple. She had seen Malyah Man in all his colours. What he was doing out there on his own in the wilderness no one knew.

She finally found Varo in a storeroom, crouching before a cupboard.

"Come on in." He made a wide sweep of his hand.

He looked wonderful to her eyes. Blazingly alive, exuding energy. What would she do if he disappeared out of her life? The pain would be excruciating.

Everything in life has its price.

She understood that. There might be a crushing price for her behaviour, although she and Varo had not slept together as her mother might have supposed. In any case, they had both become very aware of the proximity of her parents. It was agonising not to be together, but what option did they have? The high emotion of the wedding day had taken them by storm, sweeping aside their defences. Neither had set out with the intention of deliberately seducing the other. Fate had to take responsibility for that.

And here they were again.

Quite, quite *alone*.

She moved into the well stocked room, wondering what he was doing. "Can I help?"

"I'm after a powerful torch," he explained, turning his dark head to her. "The most powerful you've got."

"They're in the drawer over there." She pointed to the opposite wall of cabinets. "There are any number of powerful torches in use around the house. We have had floods and loss of power situations. The station store supplies the workforce."

"Presente!" Varo gave a cry of satisfaction, withdrawing a handheld torch. Ava could see the flashlight comprised an LED, not an incandescent bulb. This was the most powerful version of torch they had, with a solid waterproof assembly.

It suddenly struck her what he wanted the torch for. "You want to explore the hidden cave?" Her voice rose in sharp alarm.

"Ava, Ava... I will be very careful, you understand?" He put the torch down and came to her, taking her face between his hands.

"But it could be dangerous, Varo," she protested. "Dev hasn't gone all that far."

"Well, I intend to go a little further," he said, bending his head to kiss her not once but several times—tantalising little kisses promising much more. "It's in the nature of things, *mi querida*."

"Well, please leave *me* out!" Ava wrapped her arms tightly around him, revelling in his wonderful physicality. "As I told you, I'm more than a bit claustrophobic."

"But you *must* come with me," Varo insisted. "My concern for you will control my actions. I've done risky things. I've taken chances. I am a man, after all, and I will tell you I am considered a fine mountaineer. In my university days I led a team up one of the unexplored peaks of the Andes near the Chilean border. It was an unbelievable experience. I have made the ascent of active volcano Volcán Villarrica several times over the years. Thrilling, and not what *you* would consider safe. Climbers have fallen into lava pools and crevasses."

"Ugh!" Ava shuddered. "All in a day's climb?"

"Australia is different. You do not have our Andes, which as you know connect with the mighty Rocky Mountains."

"No, but we do have our Great Dividing Range," she reminded him with a smile. "I think it's the third longest in the world. I know it bears no comparison with the mighty Andes or the Rockies, but I still say exploring our cave system might be a tad dangerous even for you."

He traced the shallow dent in her chin with his fingertip. "I swear to you, Ava, I won't do anything foolish. Why would I? I will have you waiting for me."

The critical voice inside her started up again. *It could be dangerous.*

The problem was Juan-Varo de Montalvo wasn't your everyday man. A man of action, it would be nigh on impossible to stop him.

As a safety measure they had packed hard hats. Outside the cave the sun was at its zenith, blindingly hot and bright. Inside the cave the temperature had chilled. Varo donned his hard hat, shining the powerful torch around the cave. The great crocodile seemed to be slithering across the roof. The stick figures had picked up their dance.

It was quite spooky, Ava thought, shining her own torch. God knew how many tonnes of rock were over their heads. She couldn't help thinking of Joan Lindsay's famous story, *Picnic at Hanging Rock*. The hill country was ancient, its peaks eroded over millions of years. The thought of losing Varo, the man she knew she loved and her guest, sent waves of terror through her. Her heart was even bumping against her cotton shirt.

Varo looked down at her with brilliant eyes. "Give me your blessing."

She opened her mouth to say something, but no sound came out.

"Do not worry. I'll be fine. One kiss before I begin."

"You're crazy," she whispered.

"About you."

They kissed open-mouthed. His tongue traced the lovely shape of her lips. He stroked her cheek reassuringly and then moved away to the neck of the tunnel, bending low to make his entrance. She already knew there was a long narrow passageway, leading to a chamber where a tall man could stand up with his head clearing the roof by about a foot. Dev had told her that. She also knew cave systems could go on for miles. And that highly experienced cave explorers could and did get lost. But this was a man used to high adventure. Clearly their cave system intrigued him.

She sat down on the sand, her back against a smooth unpainted section of the wall. It took her several moments to realise she was holding her breath. Around her was absolute silence. She couldn't hear Varo at all. Knowing so much about the aboriginal people and their legends, their sacred places and their taboo places, she began to wonder if the all-powerful spirits thought of them as trespassers. She knew if the cave turned pitch-black she would scream her head off. Maybe she and Varo would never leave here, like the party of schoolgirls who had simply vanished from the face of the earth.

Get a grip, Ava, said the voice in her head. *Too much imagination.* No harm had come to Dev, although he'd admitted he hadn't been too keen on exploring all that far. For one thing their grandfather would have been furious if he'd ever found out Dev had made the attempt. Quite simply, Dev had been the most important person in the world to their grandfather. Even then the planned heir, over their father.

Varo wasn't feeling Ava's apprehension. Body and mind were set on establishing what lay ahead. He had spent a great deal of time exploring rocky caves and slopes. Here it didn't seem especially dangerous, although the air smelled strange—as though it had been trapped in the cave system for millions of years. And the entry tunnel was easily negotiated, even if it seemed to go on too long. He realised he was on a descending slope, going deeper into the bedrock. Twelve minutes by his watch and he was able to clamber out into a large cave, with tumbled boulders like devil's marbles acting as giant stepping stones to the cave floor. This was Dev's cave.

He trained his powerful torch on the roof of the cavern. No rock paintings here. The roof looked quite smooth, as did the walls. The action of water over the millennium? Who knew? There had been an inland sea at the centre of this great continent in prehistoric times. Surely proof was in that rock drawing of the great crocodile, the fish and the sea creatures? He was a bit disappointed, however. He wanted excitement, achievement.

The atmosphere had turned several degrees colder. He pointed the torch downwards. The sand beneath his feet appeared speckled with gold.

"Fantastico!" he breathed aloud. He knew Dev had felt he had to call a halt on his exploration at this point. *He* intended to go further, but without putting himself at risk. He was acutely mindful of Ava's anxieties. This entire area that the family called the Hill Country—the aboriginals would have another name for it, like all indigenous people—he knew to be honeycombed with caves.

He trained his torch on the next narrow opening. It would be a tight squeeze for a man his size...

Ava thought of going in after him then rejected the idea. She hated confined spaces. She didn't even like travelling in an elevator on her own. Even the best had problems. She had to trust Varo's judgement just as she had trusted Dev's.

But it was close on forty minutes now. How long should she wait? She wondered how much trusting she could fit inside her chest. Men and their adventuring, always tilting at death. Women spent more time considering the dangers and the consequences. Women were much more careful. Women wouldn't start wars.

She completely ignored the fact that she had given the tough game of polo a go. Her grandfather had protested on the grounds that it was not a fitting game for a female. Not because she might injure her precious limbs. Oh, no! She hadn't complied. She'd been rather good at polo, although naturally down some levels from the top notch. She loved horses and they loved her. She didn't think there was a horse she couldn't ride.

A bird—a hawk—swooped, and then flew into the neck

of the cave. She let out a strangled screech that matched the predatory bird's, but in the next moment it had flown out again. She jumped to her feet because she was so agitated.

Sounds came first. Then the beam of the powerful flashlight.

Thank God! Varo was coming back. Her emotions were bobbing up and down like a cork in a vat.

He all but swam out of the cave. Clear of the tunnel wall, his arms shot out sideways, as if he were taking wing.

"Varo!" Her cry was both relieved and anxious.

He was swiftly on his feet. He didn't even stop to catch breath. If a man's face could be called radiant, then it was his. "You have to come back with me," he said, yanking off his hard hat and thrusting a hand through his tousled jet-black waves. "It's *fantastico*!" He caught at her hand, the skin of his face as cold as if he'd been out in a snowstorm. "I've never seen anything like it before."

"Like what?" Despite herself she felt caught up in his excitement.

"I won't tell you. You must see. I should tell you first there's a narrow passageway that turned out to be a bit of a squeeze for me, but you'll slide through it."

"Am I free to refuse?" she asked, with humour and a trace of real fear.

"Of course. But there's no danger. I don't know about further into the cave system. There could be real danger there. One would need the proper equipment. But so far so good, as they say." He reached down to pick up her hard hat. "Here—put it on. You will be safe with me, my love. Bring your torch. You can't say no, Ava. You will be missing something."

He sounded and looked as exhilarated as she imagined Howard Carter might have looked and sounded when he opened up Tutankhamen's tomb ninety years before.

Ava took the hard hat from him, settling it on her head. With Varo beside her she could conquer her fears one by one.

"Lead the way," she invited.

In the "squeeze" passageway she felt a split second of over-whelming claustrophobia. She wanted to scream, but she didn't have enough air in her labouring lungs. What did the air smell of anyway? Bizarrely, she thought of shingle at low tide. Salt, sand, a whiff of fish and sea creatures. How crazy was that?

Just as she was about to fall flat on her stomach and stay there a minute or two, the passageway opened up.

Varo was through, reaching back for her. He pulled her out with as little effort as he might expend on a child. They were standing on a huge slab of limestone roughly ten feet square—one of many flat slabs descending to the cavern floor. To Ava's astonished eyes the huge area looked like a theatre, held up by fabulous twisting pillars The sight was so fantastic, so surreal, it almost hurt her to look. Yet she felt quite secure.

She pushed her shoulders back. Her breathing eased. Varo's strong arm was locked around her. She felt there was no space between them. She had fallen so madly in love the other versions of herself had faded into the past. This was the start of a whole new Ava.

"*Vaya!* Well?" He unfastened his headgear, then hers, dropping the hard hats on the huge slab.

His vitality was like an electric field. It sent charges siz-zling through her. "Oh, my God!" she murmured, her awe mixed with reverence. "This is utterly fantasmagorical—if there is such a word."

Stalagmites, stalactites—she wasn't sure which was which—marvellous curtain-like draperies, giant toadstools apparently formed from ochre mud, others the shape of the water-lily pads that grew in such profusion over Kooraki's billabongs and lagoons, all filled the grand space. In one area there was an organ like structure she thought might thunder if it was ever played.

The smell of the sea inside the cavern was even stronger, yet there wasn't a visible drop of water about them. No shallow pools. Certainly no underground river. They were, however, over the Great Artesian Basin. The cave was as dry as ancient bones.

"These are natural heritage objects, are they not?" Varo asked, turning his lustrous eyes on her.

She nodded in wonderment. She was finding it hard to process all she was seeing. They were holding two powerful torches, but the brightness inside the chamber was hard to explain. She looked up. The sun might have been shining through a hole in the roof of the cavern, except of course it wasn't.

"Protected by law," she confirmed. "One can't break even the tiniest piece off. Which are the stalagmites? I should know."

"The ones growing vertically from the cavern floor," he replied. "The stalactites are the curtains. See how they touch each other, forming the draperies? This wonderful scene was formed by dripping or flowing water perhaps a million years ago. Your famed inland sea?" he suggested.

"It could well be," Ava said. Her whole being was aglow. "To think it has all been here for probably thousands of years. I should think the early aboriginal tribes would have known about these caves. And the rock paintings."

"The ones that did know would have died out."

"But they always passed on their legends. And what about all the sparkles on the floor of Dev's cave?"

A smile swept his dynamic face. "Fool's gold?"

She lifted her face to the mighty organ, with shifting prisms of light bouncing off its cylindrical pipes. "Do you think we should be here?" she asked softly. "This could be a sacred site for all I know."

"Frightened, are you?" There was a pronounced tease in his voice.

"Not with you. We're together." She had never said such a thing before. Never felt like this before. "Have you ever heard the legend of Lasseter's Reef, Varo?" she asked, prompted by the mystery glitter. Opal matrix had been found on the station. But no gold-bearing quartz veins. *As yet!*

His face relaxed into his devastatingly attractive smile. "I am sorry, but no," he said gently. He was gaining enormous pleasure from her reactions, and the fact she had conquered her claustrophobia. That was brave.

"Then I'll tell you the greatest mystery of our gold fields."

"I'm listening, but let's go down." He kept an arm around her, guiding her as they descended the staircase of toppled slabs. Memory was stirring. Something he had read some-where, some time. That riveting word *treasure*!

"Debate continues to this day." Ava was staring around her in a wondering way. What would Dev and Amelia make of this? She couldn't wait to tell them. "Gold was the back-bone of the nation then. There were huge gold strikes all over."

"I've heard."

"Prospectors came from all over the world." She crouched over the extraordinary "lily pads", awestruck. They might have been cast in stone over a living plant. "Harold Lasseter was a young prospector who became hopelessly lost when he was prospecting for rubies in the MacDonnell Ranges."

"That's the Red Centre?" Varo asked. He was looking

forward to seeing the great desert monuments. Ava *had* to be with him.

Ava nodded. "It was long ago—around the late 1890s. My family, the Langdons and the Devereauxes, were here, pioneering the cattle industry. Anyway, Lasseter claimed when he was found, starving and dying of thirst, he had stumbled across a fabulous reef of gold and taken samples. An Afghan camel driver actually saved his life. Three years later, restored to health, he went back with a surveyor. They claimed to have re-found the reef, taking bearings with their watches."

"Only to find when they got back to civilisation their watches were incorrect?" Varo guessed.

"You've heard this story," she said wryly.

Varo only shrugged.

"Other expeditions followed, but it was all too dangerous. Forbidding territory, and the tribes were well equipped to defend their land. Spearing of the invading white man was common, which meant the Government of the day wasn't keen on sending expeditions into the desert to be killed or die of starvation and thirst."

"Okay—you tell me this so we can go and find it?" he asked, amused.

"Many people believe the reef is out there." She was speaking now in a hushed whisper.

They began to pick their way with the utmost care across the floor of the cavern, avoiding all the extraordinary formations. The bone-dry sand crunched beneath their feet.

"This is out of this world!" Ava exclaimed, enraptured by such a spectacle.

"The best news is we are quite alone," Varo said "*Finally.* I do like your parents. I enjoyed their company. But I longed for us to be together." He put out a hand, bringing her to her feet. He tugged gently on the silk scarf that tied back her hair, releasing it in a flood of gold.

"You want to make love?" she asked, on a long, voluptuous sigh.

"Need you ask?"

The expression of tenderness in his eyes almost brought her to tears. "This could be a sacred place, Varo."

"What we feel is sacred, is it not?" he asked, very gravely. "You fall in love with me. I with you."

She expected her inner voice to step in. Only it didn't. There was nothing to explain this. Nothing to gainsay it either.

All was quiet. The fantastic formations might have been ancient statues, quietly watching on. This was a dream, not a nightmare.

"Come here to me."

Varo took her torch from her, set it down beside his so the combined lights spread their illumination all through the cavern. There were no dark shadows, only wondrous natural sculptures. Could any woman resist an invitation like this?

Ava buried her face against his chest. "You *made* me love you."

"Is that the start of a song?" he mocked gently.

She lifted her head, her heart in her eyes. "Neither of us planned this, Varo. I wasn't ready for it. It's all happened so very, very quickly."

"Can one call *destino* a bad thing?" His deep dark voice crooned gently against the shell of her ear.

"Destiny?" That was the way she saw it. "I'm in love with you, Varo," she admitted freely. "I'm in love with a man from another land."

Emotion made his voice rough. "I will never leave you, *mi querida*. You will never leave me."

"How can that be—?" She started to speak, but his mouth covered hers so passionately her heart contracted. She was consumed.

"You understand it will take a little time?" Slowly, almost dazedly, he lifted his head.

"I *will* be a divorced woman, Varo." She felt compelled to point that out. "Your parents, your sisters, your family might not approve of a divorced woman in your life."

"My family will have their say of course," he admitted without hesitation. "All families do—especially one as close as mine. But *I* make the decisions. Besides, you are an angel."

"No, I'm not!" Her jewel-like eyes blazed. She didn't want Varo to put her on a pedestal.

"Not you're not!" he agreed gently in his throat. "You're a woman. All woman. *My* woman."

His dark, dark gaze was ardent, diamond-bright. In one smooth motion he had her blue and white striped cotton shirt free of her jeans, easing it off her shoulders.

Was it her over-active imagination or was the cavern lit in a golden glow?

"You're feverish!" His mouth was gliding all over her satin smooth exposed skin. Shirt and flimsy stretch lace bra had since fallen to the sand.

"On fire," she whispered back.

Very tenderly he lowered her to the sand. It didn't feel crunchy at all. It felt more like a velvet quilt. He couldn't leave her after this. He *couldn't*. This was not only a ravishing physical experience. It was spiritual.

Varo bent his head to kiss the tears away from her eyes. "We pick our path, my beautiful Ava. Nothing feels wrong to you, does it?" he asked with marked tenderness.

"How could anything be wrong when we are together."

Ava knew now she would put up the fight of her life to hold on to her love.

Varo.

She had been too malleable too much of the time. Too afraid to reach out. She wasn't there yet. But she would be. That was her vow.

CHAPTER EIGHT

HE HAD little difficulty chartering a flight to Kooraki Station from the domestic terminal at Longreach. It cost him, but Luke had never felt so determined on something in his entire life. He wanted Ava back. He was going to get her back. And, by God, he would make her suffer when he did. Not physically—never physically. He was after all a gentleman. But he had special psychological powers over his wife.

She had as good as accepted she hadn't been a good wife to him. In his world, the *real* world, the *man* reigned. He had quickly learned how to control Ava's spirit. She was too gentle by far, too tender, too sensitive. She had always been frightened of conflict. That old bastard Gregory Langdon with his Midas touch must be answering for a lot, he thought with intense satisfaction. Ava had been terrified of her grandfather. And she hadn't been the only one. Most people had. Except for Amelia's beautiful conniving mother, who had been left a considerable fortune by her long-time lover. Great to know she was an outcast now, shunned by all.

There was no one about when he landed. He waited on the tarmac until the pilot turned the nose of the Cessna about. Then until he was taxiing down the runway to take off. He hated flying in light aircraft. As far as he was concerned light aircraft had a bad reputation.

Two sulphur-yellow helicopters were grounded to the right of the giant silver hangar emblazoned on its roof with the station's name. He strolled over to a station Jeep, saw with relief the keys were in the ignition. Why not? Who was there to steal the vehicle? The Langdons ruled this Outback kingdom. James Devereaux Langdon, his revered brother-in-law, wore authority like a cloak. Quickly he pitched his suitcase in the back, then climbed into the driver's seat. No way was he going to walk up to the homestead. It was a hell of a distance, and he had always hated the dry inland heat. The Jeep was a gift.

He had a plan in place. The Argentine was still there— a favoured guest. Elizabeth and Erik Langdon were back in Sydney. Karen always had kept him well informed. Pity she wasn't more attractive. Well, she *was* in her way, and extremely smart, but her fine-boned featured face was a bit too much on the hard side. Actually, Karen Devereaux was a genuine bitch. No friend to Ava, but she had come in handy over the years when he needed information.

His idea was not to confront his wife in anger. Dear me, no! He had to get this de Montalvo guy on his side. Perhaps Ava hadn't done anything wrong. Perhaps the Argentine hadn't done anything wrong either. To split them, thus bringing any budding relationship to a halt, he intended pouring his husbandly woes into Montalvo's ear. By and large *he* was the innocent party. He, the long-suffering husband. Ava had led him an excruciating emotional dance. Ha-ha—not the tango. He had accepted all the punishment she had meted out. The thing was he loved her. He adored her. He saw no life, no future without her.

He had few peers when it came to winning people around. He was, he knew, an unsung genius. He had a top job. No one was about to steal his wife away from him. Certainly not a South American gigolo.

The housekeeper was at the front door to greet him. No, *greet* wasn't the right word, he quickly saw. From the expression on her dark-skinned face she was tossing up whether to slam the door on him or reluctantly admit him. She ought to be dismissed.

Her liquid black eyes bored into his. "Ms Ava is not at home," she announced, clearly challenging him to dispute it.

For a moment he felt like giving her a good shove out of his way. Rude bitch! He had encountered her before. "That's all right," he returned very mildly, as though he had plenty of time. "Where is she? It's Mrs…isn't it?" He couldn't for the life of him think of her name.

She didn't supply it. For God's sake, didn't she know how a housekeeper was supposed to behave?

"I'm hoping to stay for a few days," he said, preparing to sweep past this formidable woman. "My wife and I need to talk. Perhaps you could show me my room? When are you expecting my wife back?" he asked, playing up the *wife* for all he was worth. They had been estranged for more than nine months now and time was running out. This surprise visit was very serious.

The woman gave a twirl of her hand. "I have no idea. Miss Ava is not on Kooraki at this time. She is showing a guest around Alice Springs and our most famous desert monuments."

He forced an untroubled smile. "That's nice. The Langdons are extremely hospitable people. I'm in no hurry. I have a week off to expedite a couple of outstanding matters. I'd like to see my room now, if it's no trouble? It was a long trip getting here. Lunch would be nice—in, say, an hour?"

With hidden amusement he watched the housekeeper inhale hard through her wide nostrils. But what could she do? Throw him out? He *was* Ava's husband, after all. He was being perfectly respectful. He had deliberately used the word *expedite*. To all intents and purposes he was here to agree to a divorce, throwing no objections into the pot. It was all politics. He spent much of his time pretending this and that.

Ava and Varo flew back into Kooraki late afternoon the following day. Nula Morris hadn't wasted a moment leaving a message for Ava at the hotel where they'd been staying—in separate rooms—so they were prepared for a confrontation of some sort. Luke Selwyn would never have dared to set foot on the station with the Master of Kooraki at home, but Dev and Amelia were currently in Rome.

To Varo it was quite simple. He was here to keep Ava from all harm. He wasn't concerned about Ava's husband. From what he had gleaned from Dev and Amelia, and around the station, Luke Selwyn was held in poor regard. He had been judged by one and all as an unsuitable husband for Ava. They had all known Ava had been desperate to escape an unhappy home life. But her hopes of happiness had sadly unravelled along the way.

Nevertheless Varo had not been prepared to meet such an outwardly pleasant and good-looking man. He resembled an English actor whose name eluded him—the one with the floppy fair hair and earnest blue eyes. It was obvious Luke Selwyn was still deeply emotionally involved with his beautiful wife. Indeed, when he had come downstairs to greet them his blue eyes had momentarily shone with tears. He appeared to be taking Ava's wish for a divorce with stoicism, and a considerable degree of pain that he sought to hide—or was going all out to create that impression. There was no sign whatsoever of fuming jealousy, hostility, let alone paranoid rage. Not that Ava had spoken out against her husband. He thought Ava was prepared to shoulder her own share of blame.

Only it couldn't be easy to throw one's husband aside, jettison a marriage. Selwyn would have to be some sort of ogre figure. He certainly didn't present himself as one. And he had risked coming out here, where he clearly wasn't wanted. But then things happened in a marriage. For better or worse.

Ava flatly refused to sit down opposite her husband for dinner. "We're finished, Luke," she told him firmly. "Why are you here?" She raised her elegant brows. She knew Luke was well into role-playing and she disapproved strongly.

"I hope it's not an inconvenience for me to come here, Ava. I wanted to say—I just wanted to clear up a few points."

He thought he looked the very picture of embarrassment to the Argentine standing at Ava's shoulder. De Montalvo was very tall and devilishly handsome, but not in any matinee idol way. He looked damned formidable. He had been hoping for a bit of a playboy. No such luck! The man had real charisma. And obviously, going on everything about him—his manner, his speech, his air of confident authority—he came from a privileged background. That was the big surprise.

Karen had spoken about de Montalvo as though his main attraction was phenomenal sex appeal. Indeed, she thought de Montalvo so sexy she could hardly contain herself. He could see the sex appeal, all right. But *daunting* was a better word. De Montalvo was no one's fool either. It would be an enormous coup to turn this man off Ava. But it was *possible*. Anyway, wouldn't a guy like that, who had it all, have a girlfriend back home? Hell, a string of girlfriends. He *was* a hot-blooded Latin, after all.

In the end Ava relented. He had been counting on that.

They were all adults, civilised people, weren't they? Dinner actually went smoothly, considering just the three of them sat down and there were so many subterranean currents. Nula was an excellent cook. He had to give her that. He was very particular about his food. And drink, of course. Kooraki maintained an excellent cellar.

For starters they were served quietly and unobtrusively with crab and mango salad and wafer-thin fresh coconut slices, followed by duck breast on a bed of hot steaming wild rice. An exquisite *millefeuille* with passionfruit curd was wheeled in for dessert. No complaints there.

Ava could put a decent meal together at a pinch, but she wasn't in the same class as her mother. But she was *so* beautiful, with her tender, angelic face. He felt like reaching out and slapping it. Not able to do that—he could just imagine how de Montalvo would react—he continued drawing the Argentine out about life in his own country as though he were really interested. They had already discussed Uluru and the Olgas, for God's sake. Been there, done that.

Of course the two of them had slept together. There was no doubt whatsoever in his mind. Ava had an astonishing *glow* about her. A luminescence that lit up her blonde beauty. Unfaithful bitch! How he didn't leap to his feet and savage them both with furious accusations he didn't know. Or perhaps he did. The upshot might have been de Montalvo knocking him flat. Instinct told him the Argentine would be quite the wrong man to cross. And he looked so damned athletic—physically superior at every level.

But did he want Ava? That was the burning question. Or did he have an affair in every part of the world he wandered into? It was hard to gauge the Argentine's thoughts. The coal-black eyes were brilliant but quite unfathomable. Surely it couldn't be an act, de Montalvo's displaying interest in what he had to say? Then again, he had been told more than once he was an excellent conversationalist. De Montalvo had even asked him if he had ever played polo. He had answered regretfully that he had never had the time. What he'd actually meant was, had he ever considered playing the game of polo he would have needed his head read. Life and limb were much too precious.

Now all he had to do was keep his cool, act brain-dead in relation to their trip together and his wife's scandalous behaviour, and get de Montalvo alone. He wasn't sure if he should play his trump card. It was a horrendous lie, and it could prove dangerous, but he suspected he might have to use it. He had to change the Argentine's opinion of Ava, who was still *his* wife. That called for drastic measures.

All's fair in love and war, old son!

Fortune smiled on him. He had to control a mad desire to fall to his knees and give thanks. By an incredible stroke of luck one of the Langdon circle—a near neighbour Siobhan O'Hare, the one who had lusted after Langdon but lost out to Amelia—took a trip over to Kooraki to visit. No doubt to find out if the honeymooners were surviving the honeymoon, he thought waspishly. Obviously hope sprang eternal. If ever the marriage broke down, the ever-faithful Siobhan would be waiting in the wings. God knew how she thought she could ever replace the glorious, voluptuous Amelia. But most women had inferior reasoning powers.

Juan-Varo de Montalvo, *hidalgo* that he was, was on hand to say hello to Ava's visitor—who, let's face it, looked at de Montalvo with a suspicion she couldn't hide in her eyes. Why was the glamorous Argentine still on Kooraki? Shouldn't he have already gone on his way?

He knew exactly the thoughts that were ticking over in little Siobhan's head. Ava was still married. To *him*. Luke Selwyn. Blue-chip lawyer. What was *he* doing on Kooraki, for that matter? Initially she had looked as though she had stumbled into a war zone, but with his natural charm of manner he had made it clear there was no animosity between him and Ava. She was permitted the sneaking feeling he was secretly devastated, but hiding it like a man.

To celebrate this wonderfully timely intervention he suggested to the Argentine they take a run around the station in the Jeep that was parked out at the front.

"Might be my last time here," he said, with a pained air of regret. "Ava said at dinner she intended taking you out to see Malyah Man?" He had found the weird sandstone monument bloody terrifying, but he had to get de Montalvo somewhere out there, where they wouldn't be interrupted. Malyah Man was ready to hand. "I could show you," he said, giving the other man a friendly smile.

Varo stared down at Selwyn, wondering what was going on beneath the convivial exterior. The man could be a sociopath for all he knew. He knew a sociopath's destructive qualities were not easily recognised. They could be charming when required. He had heard Ava's husband was a very self-centred man. Whatever Selwyn was, he knew he could handle him.

"You have a camera?" Luke asked, rubbing his chin.

"Sure."

"You might like to take photos," he suggested. "It's an incredible structure—rather like those Easter Island statues. The girls can enjoy morning tea and a chat without us around. We'll be back in little over an hour. It really is an exceptional sight."

When de Montavlo went off in search of Ava he stood in the Great Hall, rocking in his boots. He had gained valuable time with his wife's lover. He had to make the most of it. He would really like old Malyah Man to topple and fall in a great crush on the Argentine. He wouldn't mind that at all. But he knew it wasn't going to happen.

Ava wasn't at all happy Varo had agreed to go for a trip around the station with Luke. But what could she do? If she said she didn't want him to go with Luke, it might appear to him as if she had something to hide. Her way to prevent Luke from giving his side of the story.

She hesitated, her mind racing. Luke was up to no good. She knew him too well. He would be out to squeeze the last little drop of sympathy he could out of Varo. That was the role he had chosen to play. The wronged husband. Helpless to keep a wife who no longer wanted him or needed him. She came from a rich family, but now she had no sense of dependency on anyone—much less her husband. Her grand-father, thinking she would never be able to stand on her own two feet, had made her totally independent for life.

Ava's nerves were jangling. She couldn't help feeling a creeping apprehension. If Luke couldn't have her, Luke would be out to destroy her. Or her one big chance at happiness.

"Well?" Varo questioned humorously, as she hesitated.

"I had intended showing you Malyah Man myself." She tried not to show any trace of her inner agitation.

Varo shrugged. "Then Selwyn and I will go some place else. There—that's decided."

Siobhan's clear voice piped up from the seating area behind them. She could feel Ava's tension. And why wouldn't she be tense? It was obvious to her there was something between Ava and the dashing Argentine. Luke Selwyn must be feeling it too—not that she had ever liked him. But one *could* feel pity. "Oh, Malyah Man is marvellous, Varo. You must see it before you go home," she enthused.

Ava took a breath. "Well, I suppose if Luke wants to show you, then go by all means."

"Not if you're upset about it?" Varo took no heed of the overly curious neighbour. It was all he could do not to draw Ava into his arms, hold her tight against his chest.

Ava raised a smile. The last thing she should appear was anxious. Or, even worse, *guilty*. "Of course not. Don't be long."

"Just over an hour, Selwyn said."

"Lunch at one," she reminded him, turning to her uninvited guest, whose ears and eyes were agog. "You're staying, of course, Siobhan?"

Siobhan pinkened up. "Love to," she gushed. She couldn't wait to tell her mother all about this. The Argentine was so sexy she felt a throb in her own blood.

Poor old Luke!

Blazing sunlight flooded the plains. On the far side of them the jagged outline of the ancient Hill Country stood fierily against a cobalt sky. Never until the day he died would Varo forget the sublime experiences he and Ava had shared.

He had seen many extraordinary and extreme sights so far in his life, taken many adventurous journeys. He and two friends had once loaded their backpacks and climbed to the top of a spurting volcano, where they'd had to don masks and protective gear. With the same companions he had gone extreme white-water rafting in turbulent waters. He had visited Antarctica—amazing beyond belief—and the Galapagos Islands with their wonderful evolutionary marvel the giant Galapagos Turtle and magnificent marine iguanas—the only sea-going lizards in the world.

He had followed the Argentine revolutionary Che Guevara's journey on his own motorcycle, half believing in the Curse of Che. It was well documented that the Bolivian politicians and generals who had shared responsibility for his death had later met with violent accidental deaths themselves. He had visited all the wonders North and South America could offer. He had seen the great awe-inspiring desert monuments of Central Australia.

But he had never before made passionate love to a woman while lying on the velvety sand of an ancient cavern with fantastic pre-historic formations gazing down at them. It was an experience that had great meaning for him, because he knew the passion he felt for Ava was true.

Luke Selwyn's voice jolted him out of his lingering euphoria. "Almost there," he announced, with a sidelong grin. "He looks a cantankerous old bugger, Malyah Man. I know Ava was always frightened of him. But then Ava has phobias." He paused for a moment, gnawing his lip. "I love her, you know."

"Love her or want to hold on to her?" Varo asked bluntly, glancing across at Ava's husband.

"Of course I want to hold on to her," Luke freely admitted, almost banging his fist on the wheel. "What man wouldn't? She's so beautiful."

"She is. But she has many other qualities to be greatly admired," Varo clipped off.

"Of course, of course," Luke agreed at once. "She's the loveliest person in many ways. But it broke my heart that she didn't want children. I know what was at the bottom of it, of course," he said with deep regret. "For all the fact she was a Langdon, she had a miserable childhood. She was terrified of her grandfather. He was an immensely powerful, tyrannical man."

Varo felt his heart flip over in his chest. Ava didn't want children? Could Selwyn, who appeared genuinely broken-hearted, possibly lie about something like that?

He suddenly remembered how his eldest sister, Sophia,

had sworn she would never go through the experience of childbirth again after Alvaro, his nephew, had been born after a prolonged and difficult labour. Sophia, however, had changed her mind. She had brought adorable little Isabella into the world, with none of the trauma associated with Alvaro's birth. Maybe his beautiful Ava felt threatened by the pain of childbirth? Men couldn't totally understand. He had friends who had been overwhelmed by their wives' first pregnancy. Over-protective, over-anxious—living the pregnancy. He felt he might be like that too. One's wife would be the most important woman in the world.

"Are you okay?" Luke was asking with concern. "You've gone quiet on me."

"Have I? I was thinking about my sister, actually," he said, choosing his words. "You were telling me Ava doesn't want children?"

Luke took a deep breath before continuing—a man trying to calm himself. "I was. It blew me away. There was never a hint of it before we were married. I naturally assumed Ava would want children as much as I do. My parents were longing for a grandchild. But Ava's attitude firmed with every passing day. I wanted her to have counselling about it, but she flatly refused. Please don't think I didn't try to calm her, Varo. I believe she really fears childbirth. Some women do. It got to the point where I was getting a bit paranoid myself. And then we discovered she *was* pregnant. My God!" he said quietly. "I was the *enemy* from that moment. Something must have gone wrong with her contraception method. It happens. I have to confess when she told me I couldn't help but be *thrilled*. The longed-for child! I promised Ava I would do anything—everything—to support her, that we would get her safely through pregnancy together—" He broke off, overcome by emotion.

The towering figure of Malyah Man loomed ahead, but

Varo was seeing it through a blinding haze. He had to grit his teeth. Even his breathing was constricted. Out of the clear blue he was abruptly unsure of anything. He might just as well have stepped off a cliff. Ava was in his blood-stream. He had come to think of her as part of his destiny. But what did he *really* know of her? Indeed, what did she know of *him*? The two of them had been swept away by the force of their feelings. It was a classic case of the heart rul-ing the head, the fatal *coup de foudre*. Still, a big part of him was highly suspicious of Selwyn, the self-styled wronged husband.

"Let's park the Jeep first," Selwyn suggested, like a man trying to buy time. "I can't go on for the moment. I get too damned upset. Ava was the centre of my world. A child would have made us complete. I was *absolutely* certain Ava would come around. I really felt that her peculiar fears would pass. A kind of phobia, I suppose. Not all women long to have a child. Many elect to go childless these days. Some don't even want a man as soon as they become financially independent. Sorry if I'm drawing you into this, Varo," he said, with an apologetic half-smile. "But it's good to be able to talk to someone. You know—like strangers on a train. I can't talk to my parents. I wouldn't dream of talking to our friends—"

"But surely you have Karen Devereaux's ear?" Varo broke in, feeling the heat of anger but fighting it down. He wanted to grab hold of Sewlyn, drag him out of the vehi-cle, beat the truth out of him. Yet his question was asked suavely, with a touch of sarcasm.

Selwyn responded at once, as though anxious to clear that point up. "As though I'd talk to Karen about Ava!" he exclaimed, lifting one hand off the wheel and throwing it up for emphasis. "Poor old Karen has been competing with my wife all her life. She is horrendously jealous of Ava. She has every reason to be. No, I couldn't confide in Karen," he said ruefully, shaking his head, "although she likes to keep in touch. She rings me from time to time. Karen doesn't trust many people, but she trusts me."

Varo kept silent. His nerves were drawing tighter every second. He could see Selwyn wanted to tell him more. He wasn't at all sure how he would react. He would never have thought for a moment Ava might not want children. He had assumed she was a woman who loved children as he did. Now he was no longer sure of anything. He would bide his time, hear Selwyn out.

Like the vast desert monuments Uluru and Kata Tjuta, rising as they did out of the featureless plains, so too did Malyah Man. The striking sandstone pillar was set in the middle of nowhere, surrounded by grassy flats that were thickly sewn with some pink flowering succulent he later learned was *parakeelya*—an aboriginal word. The stock liked to feed on it.

"Fantastic, isn't it?" Selwyn commented, as they stepped out of the Jeep. "Ava never would come here alone."

"So you said." Varo walked to the foot of the ancient formation—probably the only remaining relic of some pre-historic plateau. He tried to keep his mind focused on the natural formation. It reminded him strongly of tribal sculpture. African or Toltec-Mayan. There was a great dignity to the extraordinary "human" head. Certainly it wasn't a welcoming figure. It was a *guardian* figure. He was sure of it.

Selwyn was somewhere behind him, obviously keeping his distance.

Varo turned around. "It seems you suffer your own apprehension?" he said with a vague taunt.

"Well, he *is* a scary-looking guy." Selwyn tried a laugh that didn't quite come off. But to prove himself he moved over to where Varo was standing. "I hope I haven't upset you?" he asked, studying the Argentine's handsome profile. It was set in stern lines.

"In what way?" Varo glanced sideways, stared the other man down.

"A man would have to be blind not to notice you're attracted to my wife," Luke offered, holding up his hands in peace.

"I would think any man that laid eyes on her would be attracted," Varo returned. He rested a reverent hand against the sandstone folds of Malyah Man's "cloak".

Luke sighed. "I just wanted you to get things right," he said. "There's so much I could tell you."

"Go right ahead," Varo invited, covering the deep stabs of anger.

Luke lowered his voice, as though talking to himself. "I have to get this off my chest, Varo. It's been killing me. You have no idea how lost and wretched I feel. I'm a man who believes in marriage. I believed in *my* marriage. I love Ava with everything I am. Body, heart and soul."

"Apparently you weren't able to convey your deep feelings to her?" Varo said, shooting his companion a derisive look.

"You don't understand." Luke rubbed fiercely at the nape of his neck. Something had stung him, dammit! "The pregnancy ended in catastrophe." His voice dropped to a hoarse whisper. "Ava—my beautiful Ava, who looks like an angel—aborted our child."

This time Varo couldn't control himself. He lashed out on instinct, grabbing hold of Selwyn by his smarting neck. "You're lying," he rasped.

He looked so daunting Luke Selwyn moaned aloud. "Please…" Luke struggled to get free, but the Argentine held him fast. He was inches taller, fitter, stronger, and his black eyes were glittering with rage. "You don't *want* to

believe it. I understand. I *have* to tell you. I refused to believe it too. Only it's too true. Ava aborted our child. She
confided in Karen. At least Karen was always there for
her. Her family don't know. I *know* it sounds appalling. It
is appalling. I realise now I shouldn't have told you. This
is something I should have kept to myself. Forgive me, but
I thought you deserved to know. I'm sorry."

Varo didn't loosen his grip. On the contrary, he strengthened it, knowing he was spinning out of control. Selwyn
was lying. It couldn't possibly be true. Ava had aborted a
child? Unthinkable. He *loved* her. He knew now he had
never fallen in love before. How could he not be shaken to
his very core?

"Varo?" Luke Selwyn's voice quaked. He had taken a risk
and now it looked as if his desperate ploy had backfired.
His heart started to thump. He had never felt so exposed.
For all he knew the Argentine was going to kill him.

Out of nowhere a hot, gusting wind suddenly blew up. It
was so fierce Luke felt a kind of desperation to find shelter.
Not so the Argentine, who seemed to be part of it all. Was
a desert storm about to roll over them? The Outback was
such a dangerous, unpredictable place.

Even as he wondered, de Montalvo thrust him away as
if he was beneath contempt.

How dared he?

Luke fell heavily, wondering if something terribly untow-
ard was on its way. His wife's lover, of all people, intended
to beat the living daylights out of him. And in the middle
of a dust storm. They might have been in the Sahara. He
could taste red dust in his mouth, clogging it, preventing
speech. He looked up, as if impelled. It was a mistake. At
that precise moment a fist-sized rock broke away from the
towering sandstone formation, sending him into a cower-
ing position. The rock appeared to hang for a split second

in mid-air, before it fell with a clunk on his head—although he was covering it, and his ears.

Hell and damnation!

He felt the throb. There was probably a horrible amount of blood.

For a second even Varo was transfixed. The wind that had gusted up so violently in the next minute had fallen away. It was a perfectly clear day. Not a cloud in the densely blue sky. He looked to Selwyn, huddled on the ground. "Are you okay?" He wasn't going to offer comfort, but he had to check on the man.

"I'm not right at all!" Selwyn yelled, spluttering and muttering invectives. "The blasted rock hit me." He staggered to his feet, holding a hand to the side of his head.

"I assure you, *I* didn't throw it," Varo said, turning to stare up at the regal desert monument. "Maybe Malyah Man didn't like what you were saying?" he said, with a hard, cutting laugh.

"Don't be ridiculous!" Luke examined his right hand. It was streaked with blood. He would have thought the blood would be more copious...

"Better get it cleaned up," Varo suggested with no trace of sympathy. "I'll drive."

"It's *hurting*, I tell you." Selwyn was now holding his head with two hands. He kept moaning, a continuing stream of colourful expletives flowing from his lips.

"Could have been worse," said Varo, giving Malyah Man a parting salute. He had seen many strange things at different times, but nothing the likes of that.

Selwyn was already sprinting away to the Jeep, obviously fearing a barrage of rocks.

I can't—won't—believe what he has told me.

Yet how could he ask her? If it were the truth she would be mortally wounded, exposed. A lie and she would be furious with him for even giving it a moment's credence. Either way, he was compelled to find out.

But what if it is true? It will change everything.

He couldn't begin to go there. There were life-changing moments along the way.

Selwyn was still moaning as they made their way into Kooraki's homestead. Ava, on trigger alert pretty well the whole time they had been away, was on hand to meet them in the Great Hall.

She wore a smile that faded the moment they entered the front door. "What on earth has happened?" She looked from Varo to her husband. She hardly recognised him. Luke stared back glassy eyed, his fair hair standing up in tufts, streaks of red dust all over his face.

"I'll tell you what happened." He drew a harsh, rasping breath. "Montalvo here seems to find it a joke. A big rock fell off that pillar. Size of a meteor, it was. It hit me on the side of the head. It could have *killed* me." Real tears glinted in his eyes.

Varo didn't mean to, but he laughed. "Actually, I really and truly believe it was Malyah Man who pitched it at you," he said, with no trace of humour. Indeed his temper was rising.

"You're saying a piece of sandstone fell off the monument? Is that it?" Ava asked, feeling sorry for the usually impeccable Luke. He looked such a mess he might have gone through a turbulent experience.

"Not *fell* off," Luke gritted. "The bastard aimed it right at me," he said, setting about putting his hair to rights. "Don't look so surprised, darling. You were always frightened of the thing."

"In *awe* of, Luke," Ava corrected, seeing Varo visibly tauten at the "darling". "I didn't think Malyah Man was *threat-*

ening. Well, not to me. But I wouldn't have offended him for the world." Ava's eyes met Varo's. "You okay?" she asked.

Something more had happened out there. She could tell. There was something *different* about Varo. She couldn't place it. But it was in the quality of his brilliant black gaze. It was as if he was looking at her with fresh eyes. Luke would do anything to sully her good name. The possibility he had attempted to do so was real. She didn't have an inkling what he might have said.

"I keep on the right side of the Ancients too," Varo said.

Ava was having trouble even thinking about Luke and his cracked head. Up until the time they had left, Luke had been playing the good guy. That alone made her stomach contract with nerves. Luke simply *wasn't* a good guy. He was a man who liked to get square. A man who would always seek revenge for the slightest hurt or word out of place. What had he said to Varo that made him look at her differently? What was there *to* say, for God's sake? She had always been gentle, respectful, restrained. She had never looked sideways at another man, even when she'd known plenty of men looked at her.

Finally she threw out an impatient hand. "Let's get you cleaned up, Luke, shall we? Is it painful?" God knew, Luke was no super-hero. He had always made a terrible patient, even with a head cold. "Do you think it might need a few stitches?"

"Of course it doesn't," Varo broke in, sounding incredulous. "It was more in the nature of a shot across the bows. Let's hope it worked."

Ava's eyes swept Varo. She dearly wanted to know exactly what Varo had meant by that, but she couldn't ask him there and then. It would have to wait for later. Or maybe she would never find out?

Luke was complaining wanly that he needed "peace and quiet". He could have his peace and quiet. He could stay the night, but she had organised the first leg of his trip back to Sydney for the following day. Station supplies were being flown in mid-morning. Luke could fly out with the freight plane. He could take care of himself after that. She still didn't know why he had come. They had discussed nothing. No doubt he was biding his time.

Luke was. He moved off in the direction of the first-aid room, comforted by the fact his ploy was actually working. He'd got the bandwagon rolling. All he had to do was sit back and watch proceedings. Innocent or guilty, it was a well-documented fact mud stuck. He could see how upset the Argentine was, even if he was doing a great job of keeping his feelings under wraps. Particular lies had a huge advantage. How could Ava ever prove her innocence? She could protest, sure. But would de Montalvo believe her? Would *anyone* believe her? He knew he had Karen on side. Karen would back him. Uphold his lie. You had to understand Karen's powerful jealousy of her cousin. *He* did. It had worked for him in the past. Lies could and did ruin affairs of the heart.

Luke felt no pang of guilt. Ava was his wife. She would take her punishment and then they could get on with life. The Argentine was a man who would want children. Probably a dozen or more. De Montalvo's perceptions of his angelic Ava had already shifted. He had almost heard the crash as Ava had fallen off her pedestal.

Serve her right!

He also blamed her for that whack on the head. People liked to pretend there were no such things as spirits and guardian figures. They should visit the Outback. He would swear he'd heard old Malyah Man make a deep throaty sound like *yahggh* as the rock began to fall. Weren't the old Kadaitcha Men supposed to have hissed that over their dying victims?

* * *

There was no opportunity for Ava to speak to Varo. Lunch was served, and Luke had recovered sufficiently to leave his sickbed. She could see he wasn't altogether happy with salad Niçoise and seared Tasmanian salmon escalopes. No starters. There was, however, a lemon tart to save the day.

Siobhan gave him lots of sympathy, thinking someone had to. The Argentine had a hard impatience etched on his stunning face. Ava was trying to hide some upset. "It's a wonder you weren't concussed," she said in a show of solidarity. Her tone was sugary at times, even cloying.

Luke frowned. "Perhaps I *am*." His injury was still hurting. He would need another couple of painkillers. He had to ready himself for a little talk with his wife. In his head he was tweaking it. All a man had to do was stick to his guns.

"One never knows," Siobhan pondered, looking towards her silent hostess. "When I was little I toppled head-first off a trampoline. Everyone thought I was fine but I had a concussion."

Luke didn't respond. He was always bored with problems outside his own.

Ava had to stop herself from sighing aloud. Siobhan was overdoing the sympathy. Was it deliberate? She could see Varo stir restlessly. The sooner Siobhan was on her way the better. She had flown over in her father's helicopter. Siobhan was Outback born and bred. A woman of the land. She would make a grazier cattleman an excellent wife. Of course she had been in love with Dev for years. Still was. Ava had been reminded of that constantly, with Siobhan's questions about the honeymooners. Ava hoped Siobhan would get over Dev soon. There had only ever been one woman for Dev. That woman was his wife.

CHAPTER NINE

Varo offered to drive Siobhan to Kooraki's airstrip, which seemed to cheer her immensely. She blushed.

Ava, however, spoilt the twosome by saying she would come too. After Siobhan had flown off home she would suggest to Varo they go for a drive. Maybe back to Malyah Man, as he appeared to be active. She was desperate to know what the barely perceptible change in his manner was all about. But it was there. The familiar easy charm hadn't been as much in evidence over lunch, although he had responded to all of Siobhan's thirty or so questions. One might have thought Varo came from an unknown part of the planet about which Siobhan knew nothing...

"All right, then. Goodbye." Siobhan smiled up into Varo's handsome face. "I expect you will be going home soon, Varo?"

"No, no—not *soon*," he responded, drawing out the *soon*, knowing Siobhan was storing up all she had seen and heard for relaying her family.

His response cut the goodbyes short.

Siobhan climbed into her Bell helicopter and in no time at all ascended into the wild blue yonder.

Ava looked at Varo, asking rather hesitantly, "Would you like to go for a drive?"

"As you wish," he answered smoothly.

It wasn't the answer she wanted. "Is something wrong?"

"Why would you think that?" he parried.

She gave a short laugh. "I've seen you in different moods, Varo. Sometimes I allow myself to believe I know what you're thinking."

"So what am I thinking now?"

A sudden uncharacteristic anger took hold of her. Her eyes flashed like jewels. "It's Luke, isn't it? What did he say to you?"

"What could he say?" Varo shrugged, not knowing which way to go with this. He would be so glad to be rid of Selwyn. He was even glad Siobhan O'Hare had flown off home.

"He sees you as a rival," Ava said hotly. They were, she realised with a shock, on the verge of their first argument. "Please don't answer my questions with a question, Varo. He said something to upset you. That seems clear to me. He may not have exhibited that side of him, but Luke is an extremely possessive man." Even the words in her mouth tasted bitter. "You didn't get into a fight, did you?"

Varo's voice was amused and disgusted. "Believe me, Malyah Man struck your husband the blow. I didn't have to do a thing."

"So you're not going to tell me?" Ava said. Her whole body felt as if it was going into a dejected slump.

He couldn't help touching her cheek. Her skin was as soft as a flower petal. He could smell the scent of her skin. Wound up as he was, he still wanted to take her in his arms, hold her body in an arc of intense pleasure tautly against him. Instead he said, "Let me get you out of the sun. We can't afford to bake your beautiful skin."

Ava didn't say anything until they were almost at the Jeep. "I don't want to go back to the house, Varo," she said in a strained voice. "Not with Luke there." This time her voice registered her disdain.

"So we go for a drive." Varo held the passenger door, waiting for her to get in before he closed it.

He took his time walking around to the driver's side. Luke Selwyn's disclosures had shocked him to the core. He couldn't deny that. At the same time he couldn't accept them either. His beautiful Ava not wanting children. Let alone cruelly terminating a pregnancy. He couldn't imagine the overriding guilt a woman might feel. But the Ava he knew seemed utterly guilt-free. One part of him wanted to tell Ava what Selwyn had said; the other part urged him to remain silent. Selwyn could be an utter scoundrel, a pathological liar. His reasoning would be if *he* couldn't have Ava no one else would. He couldn't bear to see Ava upset, the lovely colour gone from her face. But he actually feared he would do more harm than good confiding in her.

"So, where to?" he asked, putting the vehicle into gear.

She touched her slender fingers to her forehead. "Blue Lagoon," she said jaggedly. "We can sit on the bank beneath the trees. I know you're finding it hard to talk to me, Varo. And I know there's a reason. Luke told you something about me that has you terribly disappointed in me. In all fairness, don't you think you should tell me so I can defend myself?" she appealed to him.

Varo turned a grave face to her. She had a point. "I could be doing entirely the wrong thing, Ava," he said after a moment's consideration, "but I need to ask you. Have you ever been pregnant?"

Ava felt her heart jump in her breast. There was a long and awful ringing silence. Luke had told Varo she had fallen pregnant at some time? She literally couldn't speak she was trying so hard to control her outrage. "Excuse me—would I have kept that from you?" she demanded, fully communicating her anger.

"I don't really know, Ava," he answered quietly. And he

didn't. He wasn't by nature a judgemental man. And this was the woman he loved. "It is, after all, your business. I can understand if you had a miscarriage you might not like to talk about it. The memory could be too painful."

Ava was torn between bursting into tears and ordering him to stop the vehicle so she could jump out. "You hit Luke, didn't you?" she accused him. "Not that Luke wouldn't have had it coming."

"Would a jaguar swat a fly?" Varo returned bluntly. "I certainly wanted to—but, no, the rock fell away from the sandstone pillar. I watched it. For a split second it was stationary in mid-air, and then it dropped with a satisfactory crunch on your husband's head."

"My husband?" That hurt. Ava stared straight head. "He's *my husband* now?"

"He *is* your husband," Varo pointed out quietly.

"And you're my lover?" she asked with surprising fierceness. The writing was already on the wall. She was going to lose Varo. One way or another Luke had seen to that.

"I'm very seriously involved, Ava. We both know that." He turned off the main track, driving too fast towards the chain of lagoons. But what was in their way? These were the vast empty plains. Varo sensed she wanted to get out of the Jeep. He was finding it desperately confining himself.

"Involved? Is that the precise word?" Ava was losing the battle to keep her voice steady. "Not in love with? No? You prefer *involved*?"

"You haven't answered my question." The expression on Varo's striking face was unreadable. "I can understand if you kept it from me. You weren't sure how I would deal with it. How I would react."

"How you would react?" Ava exclaimed, her lovely face suddenly flushed with blood. She closed her eyes tight, shaking her head from side to side.

Varo believes Luke, that miserable, beastly liar. Don't men always stick together?

Luke was out to harm her in the most horrible way. He *knew* she had fallen in love with Varo. How could she hide it? Even she knew there was a special glow about her. Now she had to suffer for her perceived betrayal. She could picture the two of them talking out in the desert. Luke playing the tortured husband to the hilt. Varo feeling horrified and let down because she had kept such an event from him. She could see the residual anger still in Varo's brilliant eyes. If he hadn't actually made a physical attack on Luke he had erupted, not far off it.

"Stop the Jeep, Varo," she said furiously, and then made a huge attempt to lower her voice. "I want to get out. It seems you don't know me at all."

Varo ignored the order. He threw out a strong restraining arm across her breasts. "Sit still," he said tautly. "We're almost there."

Even the birds seemed to be singing melancholy songs. Ava stalked away from Varo down to the water's edge. This beautiful lagoon had always calmed her. Here she and Varo had sunk beneath its glittering emerald surface to steal heavenly kisses out of sight. She looked for a long time at the glorious flotilla of water lilies that steeped the lagoon in so much beauty. Nut grass and little wildflowers of flashing colours wove a sweet-scented tapestry, cloaking one area of the pale ochre sands. She had always thought this particular lagoon cast a primeval spell, but today it couldn't calm the tumult of her mind.

What else did Luke say while he was at it? She had been unfaithful? Not once but several times? Of course he had forgiven her. He could even have gone the whole hog and suggested he might not have been the father of the child? The child that never was.

She wouldn't put anything past Luke.

"Ava!" Varo called to her.

She turned back to where he was standing, in the shade of a line of feathery acacias. Such a wonderfully charismatic man. She loved him with all her heart. It was a hot, sultry, breezeless day. Shade would be welcome. Earlier in the day she had heard a series of muted thunderclaps that just as suddenly stopped. It was possible they would have a short, sharp afternoon shower. It might even be accompanied by a burst of hail. There were a few big, tumbled clouds appearing on the horizon in a peacock-blue sky.

"Let's sit down," Varo said, not knowing how to proceed exactly if Ava wouldn't confide in him. "I'm sorry if I've upset you."

Ava sighed deeply, thinking the wonderful harmony that had existed between them was as good as wrecked. She gave a raised right hand gesture, almost signifying defeat, and then sank onto the warm dry sand, drawing her legs up and clasping her arms around her jeans-clad knees.

Varo put out his hand, turning her head to him. His long fingers had a life of their own. They caressed the satin smoothness of her cheek and jawline. "Talk to me," he urged quietly.

Ava jerked her head away more forcefully that she'd intended. Her long blonde hair broke out of its clasp, spilling down her back and over one shoulder. "About what?" she asked bleakly.

"The truth. That's all I ask," he replied gravely.

Her eyes were gleaming with unshed tears. Luke had pushed all her buttons. He knew how she would react. Wind her up and let her go. "Which implies you believe I haven't been entirely honest with you?" she countered angrily. "For that matter, have *you* been entirely honest with *me*, Varo?" She was going out on the attack she was so overwrought. "Have I learned *everything* I need to know about you? You're nearly thirty years of age. You're not only a striking-looking man—a man who would compel the eyes of women—you're a man of strong passions, sexual vigour, high intellect. It's inconceivable you haven't had many affairs these past years, which you naturally don't want to expose. It's even possible you could have fathered a child and not known anything about it. It has happened countless times before today."

Varo too felt anger spurt into his veins. Anger Luke Selwyn's disclosures had caused to erupt. Now this! "Don't insult my good name, Ava," he said curtly. "I won't allow it—even from you. If a young woman had fallen pregnant to me she would have known to come to me. I would never desert such a woman, the mother of my child. However, no such woman exists. I've had my affairs. Of course I have. But I had come to believe I had never truly been in love."

"Past tense?" she said bitterly.

"It's not *me* I wish to talk about, Ava," he said, trapping her hand and holding it fast. "I have been entirely honest with you. I am, I hope, a man of honour. I was brought up to be. You are changing the subject."

"The subject being that I was pregnant to Luke?" she said hotly. "I lost my baby and I neglected to tell you about it? What is it you want me to say?"

"I've told you. I only want the truth."

"And you get to ask the questions?" The bitter note rang in her voice. She loved him so much and he didn't trust her.

"When did this happen?" he asked, feeling her anguish, desperate to understand.

At that point Ava totally lost it. She raged out of control. Her right hand—the hand nearest him—came up with the full intention of slapping his dark, handsome and arrogant face. Only he caught her wrist, bringing her arm down to her side.

"Let go of me." She couldn't endure his touching her. She began to struggle wildly, only he continued to hold her captive.

"Do not be frightened. I would never hurt you." Still, there was a little flame in his lustrous eyes. "I should never have asked you this."

"No, you *shouldn't*!" She managed to get in a sharp little punch to his chest.

The thought of losing him filled her with dread. But it was inevitable, wasn't it? She was doomed to losing the only man she could ever love. She didn't know what was happening to her because all of a sudden she was fighting him, her face flushed, her movements frantic. Anger and hopeless desire were mixed up inside her. Her every movement held an erotic charge. Not only to her. But to him. Their desire for each other was like a powerful drug that raced unchecked through the bloodstream.

Of course with his man's strength he triumphed. She was soon lying flat on her back, her body pinned to the sand. It felt much coarser than the velvety sand of the cave. Varo loomed over her, holding her down as easily as if she were a child.

He was breathing heavily, biding his time until the wild tumult of passion that was inside him miraculously cooled. This was Ava, and he was treating her with hard male dominance. The tiny top button of her pink cotton shirt had come undone. As she struggled so did the next. Now her lacy bra was exposed, and the shadowed cleft between her white breasts. His head was swimming. Her body was exquisite. He needed it so badly he almost felt like pleading for it.

"Are you going to let me up?" Her clear voice challenged him. This was a new side of Ava.

"The moment your anger passes," he announced very tensely. "A woman has never attempted to slap my face before."

"Even when you badly needed it?"

A violent hunger was washing through her. She wanted him to take her. Drive into her. Leave his brand. No way could she deny it. She was simply playing sex games. Desire was never far from them—even now, when there was so unexpectedly furious anger. The fury was actually inciting them. And it wouldn't go away. It was pumping strongly through both of them. She thought she couldn't stand it, but her body's response was just the opposite.

Still holding her arms, Varo sought her beautifully shaped sensuous mouth. He kissed her deeply, passionately, until she stopped struggling and was quiet while his hands moved over her. She should have been shamed by her surrender. Instead her senses were so exquisitely sharpened she abandoned herself to this feverish sexual onslaught. He was immensely desirable to her. Her arms came around him. Locked.

I'll never let you go.

The reasoning part of Varo was stunned by his intense hold on her delicate woman's body. Only she was egging him on, glorying in his tight embrace, even if they both remained grimly silent. There were no tender words of love. Tenderness had no place here. The hunger was boundless; the opportunity to make the other suffer as they suffered...

They were naked, their limbs tangled, bodies forming, re-forming, responding to their own rhythms that nevertheless matched perfectly. Her long blonde hair was wildly mussed. Together they were caught in a tempestuous love dance with a total lack of inhibition, willing slaves to the senses. But what kept Ava from screaming out how much she loved him? What kept Varo from responding with great

ardour how much he loved her? Both were stubbornly holding on to the raw hurt and confusion Luke Selwyn had
sparked.

They were one body. He brushed hard against the swollen
bud of her clitoris, augmenting the pleasure. Then he was
buried so deep inside her she gave an involuntary cry that
swiftly softened into satiated little gasps. At such a crucial
point, when nothing else existed outside of the pounding
waves of pleasure and excitement, she could do nothing
other than cry out his name.

Varo was unable to control his own massive response,
his thrusting deep, his possession of this woman total. He
felt as if his whole being was going out of him into her.

Above their heads the sun filtered down through the
trees. And still neither of them spoke.

When Ava was finally able to get to her feet she had to
lean against him for support. "At least I know you want me,"
she said, her voice low-pitched and trembling with emotion.

She was astounded at the wild abandon with which she
had responded to Varo's lovemaking. It couldn't have been
wrong because it had felt so right.

"As you want me," he rejoined. "Forgive me if I was a
little too rough."

She gave him a soft look. "I was as caught up as you,
Varo. Just give me a minute and we'll go. I have the feeling
we could get a heavy shower of rain. Maybe even hail."

"Let's hope so," he said tautly. He kept one arm around
her waist, absorbing her body heat. "I for one need cooling
down."

We were so happy!

Ava drew back her hair, fastening it once more with the
gold clasp. Finally she looked up, regarded him with the
glitter of tears in her eyes. "It's all so sad."

The greatest part of him wanted to tell her he loved her,

adored her. She was his woman. He would never let her go. His fears were too dominant at that moment. Difficult to accept Ava might fear having children. But that could be handled with lots of tender loving care and support. And the rest? He couldn't bring himself to reveal anything more Selwyn had said. In fact he believed in his heart it was a lie.

"You ought to talk to me, Ava," he said, pinning her sparkling gaze. "Not now. But later." Varo was striving for a detached calmness he did not feel. His desire for her would never abate. Nevertheless he said, "Both of us need a little time to cool down and reflect."

Ava turned away sharply. Her body was still throbbing. Her nipples, her breasts, her sex. She would simmer for hours. It was a new Ava Varo had set loose. A new woman he had called forth. She had lost too much time dissociating herself from her painful past. Her defeats were many. Her triumphs were to come. Nothing was going to stop her having it out with Luke. She would even holler at him if she had to. She—ever so peaceful, confrontation-hating Ava. She felt shame for how biddable she had been. A great deal of it had to do with her childhood. She was a woman now.

They both got splashed with rain and light hail as they ran from the Jeep to the short flight of front steps. Ava paused, shaking the quickly melting hail from her hair. The strong smell of ozone was in the air. Both of them had remained quiet on the journey back from the lagoon. Both knew much had to be said.

Luke watched them return. He stood at the French doors of his guestroom—not as large or as handsomely furnished at the spacious room he and Ava had always occupied, he thought with fierce resentment. He would get square. He would go back and have more of a rest before he showered,

dressed and went down to dinner. He was actually looking forward to it. Knowing Ava as he did, she would have
reacted to any accusations de Montalvo might have made
with her usual pained silence. Ava was all politeness. She
couldn't assert herself for love or money.

He didn't have to do a damned thing. All he had to do
was bide his time. The Argentine wouldn't waste a moment
getting himself organised to leave Kooraki and the beautiful Ava behind. Before the separation time was up he was
convinced he would have his wife back. With more revenge
to come. Ava had let him down very badly. How could she
avoid punishment? Subtle, of course. He had learned exactly
how to manipulate her. Not that he hadn't had *his* affairs,
but there was no question his wife could have one and get
away with it. Punishment had to fit the crime.

Some time later, when Ava burst in on him, he looked
up with genuine astonishment. "You could knock," he said,
displaying his annoyance.

At the sight of him lounging on the bed Ava's fury in-
creased. "You were *not* invited to this house, Luke," she
said. "You are *not* a guest. We are separated. I am filing
for a divorce. All this is known to you, yet you came here.
Now I know why. To cause me as much pain as you possibly could."

"Don't imagine you don't deserve it," he said in his cold-
est voice, rising slowly from the bed. He would never forgive her for what she had done, but he now felt a driving
sexual hunger. Ava had never really given herself to him.
He knew that. He knew he had never truly aroused her.
Something inexplicable to him. He had no such trouble with
other women. She looked fantastically beautiful, as though
she had suddenly stepped down from her white marble pedestal to become *woman*.

"I never deserved *you*," she said, her remarkable eyes

flashing. "I've arranged for you to fly out with the freight plane tomorrow, Luke, so you might as well do your packing tonight. The plane arrives at midday. It doesn't take long for the station supplies to be unloaded. Be ready."

Her fierce ultimatum only served to increase his rage. "You're not serious, are you, my darling?" he asked with a disbelieving sneer. "You're my wife, Ava, and don't you forget it."

"Don't dare to threaten me," Ava warned, keeping her sparkling gaze on him. "I want you *out*. If you don't choose to go quietly, I assure you I'll have you thrown out."

"By your lover?" He moved threateningly towards her.

"There will be no need to involve Varo," she said with disgust, not falling back a step as he'd expected, but holding her ground. "Any man on the station would be happy to do it. No one has any time for you, Luke. They never did. I blinded myself to your faults. You kept your true form well hidden until after the wedding ceremony. I've paid for my mistake."

"No, you haven't!" he exploded, feeling a rush of hate and hunger. "You seem to forget I could easily raise objections to your filing for divorce. Why, the separation time isn't even up and you're having it off with another man. Shame on you, Ava."

She laughed at the hypocrisy of it. "The shame is all yours, Luke. You told Varo I had a pregnancy that ended in miscarriage. That was a lie."

He came to a halt, like a statue. "And how exactly are you going to prove that?" he asked, wondering what had possessed her all of a sudden. The change in her seemed profound.

"I would think a medical check-up might do it," she retorted. "I have *never* been pregnant, Luke. I didn't want a child with you."

"But, my darling wife, you confided in Karen," he pointed out, his voice dripping acid. "Don't you remember? Karen surely will. She was as shocked as I was. Angelic old you! You have well and truly blotted your copybook. Karen knows the story."

Ava visibly paled. So he had drawn her cousin into his web. "Even Karen would stop short of telling such a lie for you," she said hardily, praying it would be true.

"Only it *is* no lie." Selwyn kept his eyes on her. "Karen suspected. You simply confirmed it. I was *thrilled* you were carrying our baby. But you aborted it, didn't you?"

Ava was seized by a pain so bad it was agony. "You told Varo I *aborted* my baby?" she cried, blazing with anger. "I don't believe it."

"Didn't he mention it?" Luke asked silkily, shaking his fair floppy head. "I suppose not. I think he was much too shocked to bring up that sad fact. He'd be Catholic, wouldn't he? Practising, no doubt—and his entire family, with their Spanish background. But you did it, didn't you? At some time we all have to take responsibility for our actions, Ava."

"Who would do this kind of thing?" Ava implored. "You disgust me, Luke. You're a truly bad man." Her voice fell away to a whisper.

Heartened, he went to her, grasped her strongly by the shoulders.

She broke away, stepping back sharply. "Keep your hands off me," she warned, very deliberately.

This was too much to tolerate. His meek, vulnerable Ava, blazing like a firebrand. "Ava, I love you," he said, injecting high emotion into his tone. "I understand your shame, your sense of guilt. You did a terrible thing. And the worst part is there was no great pressure on you, Ava—no extenuating circumstances. You weren't single, on your own with little or no money, no support. You had me and my family.

You had a choice and you chose very badly. You *know* you should be punished. What goes around comes around. You need de Montalvo to believe you. Swallow your story. But he won't. He's no fool. Okay, you let him seduce you. You've had your little bit of illicit excitement. Frankly, I didn't think you had it in you. You're such a frigid little thing."

"Not with Varo," she pointed out with pride. "And it hasn't been a case of illicit excitement, Luke. I'm deeply in love with him."

"Rubbish!" Luke exploded, seeing a red mist before his eyes. "Mark my words, you pathetic creature, de Montalvo will very soon be on his way. You're damaged goods, as the saying goes."

Ava was silent a moment longer. "Men *have* caused damage in my life," she admitted in a low voice. "My grandfather...even my father separating from the mother I loved. We weren't able to go to her. Grandfather stopped that. And *you* have done me damage, Luke. You have very dark places in you. You're a narcissist. *Your* needs are the most important thing in the world to you. You don't love me. You don't know anything about love. I entered into a precipitate marriage against all good advice. You enjoyed controlling me. You enjoyed marrying a Langdon—such cachet!"

Ava stepped forward, adrenaline coursing through her. Without another moment of hesitation she hit her husband spontaneously across the mouth. She had known in her bones Luke would provoke her into some sort of action.

Luke was genuinely shocked. He had not been expecting any such action from her. Their life together had been free of physical confrontation. He had played the psychological game. The cat and the mouse. Only the mouse had at long last found its roar.

The blow wasn't heavy, but the antique ring Ava frequently wore had managed to split his lip. He reared back

from her, as astonished as if she had morphed into a virago.
"Are you *mad*?" he exploded, unable to believe meek and
mild Ava had done this.

"Far from it. I've never had this sense of power. It's great.
You tried so hard to rob me of all confidence, Luke. That's
the ugly side of you." She picked up a handtowel he had left
on the bed and threw it at him. "Don't bleed on the carpet.
And don't attempt to come down to dinner. I'll have a tray
sent up. I mean what I say, Luke. I want you off Kooraki
midday tomorrow. I never want to lay eyes on you again."

She went to sweep past him—only in a burst of over-
whelming rage he grabbed her.

"I'm the only man you've got," he gritted, close to
screaming. There was a wild look in his eyes. "I'm your
husband—get it?"

That wild look should have made her very nervous indeed, but it didn't. "Let me go," she said, ice-cold.

Luke's good-looking face went white with fury. He shook
her hard, much the stronger of the two. "Do you really think
I'm going to let you make a fool of me?" he shouted. Then
an odd smile spread over his face. "I'm a lot more dangerous than you think, my darling." He began to rock Ava in
his arms. "No way can you leave me, Ava. Till death do us
part, remember?" One of his hands closed painfully over
her breast. "I won't be going tomorrow. But the Argentine
will. You must take your punishment. Then we can get on
with life."

Varo had had no intention of allowing Ava to confront her
husband with no back-up from him. She had been adamant
about his not accompanying her, which was fair enough,
and he had made it appear he acquiesced when his true intention was to hold himself in readiness some place nearby.
He knew the layout of the house well by now. He would

take the rear staircase to the gallery. He knew which room Selwyn was in.

Selwyn had deliberately tried to sabotage the relationship between Ava and himself. He had divulged Ava's secret, determining the relationship would quickly burn out. Selwyn wanted his wife back. No one could blame a man for that. But Selwyn wasn't a man. No one who had come close to him would think that. Malyah Man had meted out what could be taken as a genuine warning. Selwyn was *trouble*.

He'd given Ava a good five minutes to mount the main staircase and walk the short distance to Selwyn's guest-room, which was at the far end of the west wing, then made his move. His whole being had felt electric with tension. Even his scalp had prickled. He'd had only one purpose. That was to keep Ava from danger.

At the top of the staircase he'd heard voices. He had seen with gratitude that the door of Selwyn's room was very slightly ajar. Ava had evidently thought it wiser to leave it that way. In his mind he had Selwyn ripping into Ava with his accusations.

Silently he'd moved the short distance to stand just to the side of the heavy mahogany door with its ornate brass knob. Selwyn had been speaking. He'd heard him very clearly.

"Karen suspected. You simply confirmed it," he was saying. "I was *thrilled* you were carrying our baby. But you aborted it, didn't you?"

Selwyn had laughed suddenly with what Varo thought was venom and violence.

My God, was it true then? Was he about to learn the stark facts?

Ava hadn't responded. Perhaps overcome by her feelings, the trauma she had suffered. Then all of a sudden she had exploded. "You told Varo I *aborted* my baby?"

There had been rage in it, but to his ears it had sounded like righteous rage. She'd been utterly incredulous. Was this the most terrible revelation of her whole life brought out into the open, or was it Selwyn's monstrous lie?

Ava had gone on the attack. The attack of the innocent, not the guilty. He had wanted to cry out in triumph. He'd wanted to applaud. An enormous burden had been lifted from his shoulders. Instead he'd stood there, awaiting the right moment when he would thump on the door, then enter without permission.

Selwyn's accusations had continued to stream out. Ava had called him "a bad man". Her voice had been barely audible but the tones were heartfelt. In the next breath she'd switched to a shout.

"Keep your hands off me."

Time to move in on them, Varo had thought grimly. Selwyn was in full flow. He'd called Ava—beautiful, passionate Ava—*frigid*. Anger had welled up in him until he'd heard Ava's impassioned statement like a momentous declaration.

"I'm deeply in love with him."

In love with me! That's brilliant!

Selwyn had put up his worst, and Ava had had her chance to respond. Varo had found himself hanging on her every word. She'd sounded strong, independent. He had felt the fierce pleasure of pride in her. That was what Selwyn would hate—a strong, independent woman. He wanted a woman to control. Ava had broken free of her chains.

Perhaps he should not intervene, but walk quietly away. She was handling the situation on her own.

He was almost at the top of the staircase when he'd heard Selwyn roar, "Are you mad?"

It was followed by Ava's ice-cold retort, "Let me go!"

In a flash he turned back, understanding Ava was in

need of him. He threw open the door so violently it crashed against the wall, rattling a valuable *famille noir* Chinese porcelain vase that miraculously didn't fall over and break. Only who would have cared? Ava was grappling with the brute of a man she had married for all the wrong reasons. He had his hands clamped around her white neck. God, was he trying to *strangle* her?

Varo swooped, his black eyes glittering, his power-ful shoulders hunched forward like a heavyweight boxer waiting his moment to unleash his strength. Selwyn was howling now, knowing he was trapped—moreover by a man who looked as if he was about to kill him.

"She had it coming!" he panted. "Everything I told you is the truth."

He got no further. A heavy fist slammed into his ribs, knocking the breath out of him and slamming him back against the French doors.

"Get up." De Montalvo's voice was deadly quiet.

Blood was oozing from Selwyn's lip after Ava's unprec-edented attack. Now he faced possible cracked ribs. He threw up his hands as if in defeat.

Concern over what might happen lent Ava strength. She clamped her two hands around Varo's hard-muscled arm. "Leave him, Varo. Please do what I say. He's not worth it. He'll be out of here by tomorrow. I'll lock him in."

She meant it. She wasn't going to have Luke free to wan-der the house. He wouldn't get out through this door. He wouldn't dream of trying to scale the front façade. He was no mountaineer.

A hard edge was in Varo's voice. "Why don't you let me teach him a lesson?" he rasped.

"I'll have you up on an assault charge," Luke the lawyer suddenly yelled, his expression ugly.

A voice at the back of his mind was telling him Ava

would always come to his rescue. Though no woman would ever measure up to him. Few men either.

"Don't make me laugh!" Varo bit off. "What do you suppose the law would make of a man who attempted to strangle his wife? Can you see the red marks on Ava's neck, you brute? I am witness. I will call the staff to testify. You don't deserve Ava. You never did. Haven't you learned that by now?" He took several steps closer to Luke, who recoiled.

"Don't come any nearer."

"Varo, we don't want more trouble. Leave him." Ava felt her anxiety growing. She knew in her bones she couldn't find a way to Varo. He was tremendously upset.

"This poor excuse for a man doesn't deserve pity," he said with utter scorn. "What if I hadn't been there, outside the door? It doesn't take long for a man to strangle a woman. Particularly a mad man." The tension in his body was like a tightly coiled steel spring. "Get up, you gutless worm."

Luke Selwyn didn't do guts. He remained where he was, holding a hand to his ribs and making weird whimpering sounds.

Varo apparently couldn't care less. He stepped forward and gave Luke a clip across the head. "Count yourself lucky!" he exclaimed. "I believe Ava is the one who should press charges. It would and should end your career."

Luke looked past the menacing Argentine to Ava. "You wouldn't do that?" he asked, like a man amazed. "I'm your husband. I wouldn't have hurt you. I was only trying to shake sense into you."

To his horror, he received another clip over the head. "Strangle, you mean. You're on your knees, so apologise to Ava," Varo told him harshly.

Apologise? Never!

"Can't hear you," Varo said.

"Oh, God, leave him. It's not worth it." Ava's low, mellow voice had turned hoarse. She touched an involuntary hand to her bruised neck.

At that telling hoarseness Varo's strong hand came out, ready to clip Selwyn again.

"Varo, *please*. Leave him for my sake."

Varo gave her a brilliant sideways look. "I will and I am," Varo insisted. "But first the apology. Go ahead, Selwyn. While you're at it, admit your lies. You do realise you're in a very bad position indeed?"

Selwyn was silent.

Varo turned to Ava. "Looks like he's not going to do it. Ah, well!" Contempt was in his face as he stared down at the other man.

Selwyn didn't do bravery either. He broke into a choked apology without actually admitting he had lied. "I only did it because I love you, Ava. I hope you realise that?"

"Thank you, Luke," Ava said. "Tons of self-pity, no genuine remorse. The sad thing is you believe you're a good person when you're a man who knows nothing about love or even empathy. You have no capacity for it. You'll find painkillers in the bathroom cabinet. Take a good long bath. I want you off Kooraki. The chapter in life we shared is *over.*"

They were almost at the door when Luke, now up and swaying on his feet, made a final attempt to inflict more wounds and more doubt. "Ask Karen if you want to know the truth," he said, addressing Varo directly. There was a gleam of triumph in his eyes. "Women—even angel-faced women like Ava—are seldom what you think they are. What I told you should be enough to stop you from making a terrible mistake. Heed my warning. Take the path I suggest and see where it leads." He flashed Varo a smile that had nothing to do with friendship or warmth.

Varo didn't smile back. "It's important you stop now, Selwyn," he warned, looking very tense. "It's possible you may have a cracked rib or two. What about a broken nose?"

Luke's moment of feeling back in control crumbled. He had no reply to that. Ribs were one thing. A broken nose would seriously affect his good-looks. He was a man women noticed.

Luke, the king of lies, Ava thought bleakly. *Luke, the rotten liar.* He had taken lying to new heights. The truly depressing thing was that liars had a long history of being believed.

A familiar sick feeling grew in her stomach. Varo *wanted* to believe Luke was a pathological liar, but had all his suspicion fallen away? Luke had had a lifetime of practising lying. Practice had made him very convincing. She fancied she saw an element of doubt in Varo's dark eyes. If he made the decision to speak to Karen she knew she would never recover. Karen was no benevolent soul. Karen harboured the demon jealousy. She had always been Luke's ally in the past. Even so Ava thought her cousin, connected to her by blood, would not go so far as to condone such an enormous sick lie.

Right now all that mattered to her was that Varo believed in her innocence. Where would they be without trust? Trust between two people who loved each other was crucial.

Luke was locked up for the night. A generous tray had been sent up, so there was no danger of his dying of starvation. Another tray was delivered at breakfast.

When Luke's eyes locked with those of the formidable housekeeper, who clearly hated him, he began to wonder if she might have put something in his food. The orange juice tasted a bit funny. He left it aside.

He was burning up inside with fury. As soon as he got

back to Sydney he would arrange to meet Karen; probably he'd take her to dinner if he was fit enough. Put a spin on what had happened. He fully expected Karen to lie for him. He had always had a way with women. Even the strongest of them were weak. Even now he couldn't believe Ava, his wife, no longer loved him.

Give her time, said the voice in his head.

He could almost tell the future in his guts. The Argentine would go away. fade right out of the picture. His accusations would stick. He just *knew* he would have the last word.

Right or wrong, good or bad, Ava's mind was resolved on a single purpose. She had to ask Varo what he intended to do. She wanted a straight answer. If he intended to consult Karen—and even without telling her Karen would soon let her know—she could rule out her heart's desire. Varo would go. And he would go fast. Varo wouldn't be the first man to be blinded by lies. Up until now their hearts had been ruling their heads. Luke's poisonous intervention had changed all that. Luke had brought them to the *big* question.

Did Varo trust her or not?

Varo escorted Luke to the airstrip. He fully intended shoving Selwyn on the freight plane, standing by to make sure he didn't attempt to get off. From the moment they'd get inside the Jeep Selwyn had started up again.

"Beautiful women have a great deal of power. Remember that. They attract sympathy even when they don't deserve it. Men are always the losers. They lose their wives. They lose their kids."

Varo had turned to glance at him. "You never give up, do you?"

"Of course I don't. And you seem to forget I am a practising lawyer. A very good one."

"And you came close to being a criminal. You'd better remember that. You may have missed the bruises on Ava's neck, but no one else did. They will all come forward to speak out against you. I can understand in a fashion why you tried so hard to convince me of your lies, but I assure you I have no need to check out your story with Ava's cousin. I was standing outside your door earlier than you think. It wasn't difficult to believe Ava might have suffered a miscarriage and didn't want to speak about it. Impossible to believe she had her pregnancy terminated."

"Listen—"

"Be quiet now," Varo warned, his mouth twisted with distaste. "In a very short space of time Ava will apply to the court for a divorce. The separation time is almost up. You will offer no resistance. You may harbour a sick desire to hurt her, but you never will. Ava has a powerful brother. And she has *me*."

An hour passed. It was evident Varo had driven off somewhere to think. Ava walked through to the kitchen to have a word with Nula, who was waiting to prepare a late lunch. "I have to go for a walk, Nula," she said.

The housekeeper looked at Ava with concern. Ava was very pale and the marks around her lovely white neck stood out in the first flush of bruising. "A walk where?"

"Oh, just around the garden," Ava said vaguely. "Don't worry about lunch. Varo seems to have gone for a drive. We can have a sandwich and a cup of coffee later."

Ava tried for a smile. Then she walked away.

What had delayed Varo was his offering assistance to the two station hands who had been allotted the job of off-loading the station supplies. At first they seemed a bit embarrassed, he supposed because he was a guest, but he took no notice. Three pairs of hands were better than two. Besides, he liked to talk to them about what they did on the station.

When he returned to the house, Nula told him before he even had time to ask that Miss Ava had gone for a walk in the garden. It wasn't any city man's idea of a garden. It was bigger, in fact, than the gardens of Villaflores, which were extensive. No matter—he would find her. He would find her wherever she was. At the ends of the earth. He had come to this extraordinary country for the wedding of a friend. He had found a woman who had caught instantly at his heart and at his imagination. He had found his future wife.

Ava heard a man's footsteps crunching on the gravelled path. Instinctively she opened her mouth to call, "I'm here, Varo. On the stone bridge." This was it. Decision time.

Varo lost no time changing direction. He had come to know the Full Moon Bridge well. It spanned a man-made pond where the great buds of white lotus flowers slowly opened, their giant leaves almost reaching the base of the semi-circular bridge. The sun blazed out of an Outback sky of intense sapphire, lending emerald-green waters a blazing patina of gold.

Ava was standing in the middle of the bridge, gazing down at the glittering water adorned with the great gorgeous blooms. He went to call out an apology because he was a bit late for lunch, only she turned to him as he approached—such a sad, serious expression on her face.

"Ava, what is it?" His heart rocked.

"I thought you might have gone off to think," she said, lifting her remarkable blue-green eyes to him.

"Think about what?" He snaked an arm around her back, letting it fall to her narrow waist.

Slowly he led her off the bridge to one of the small

summerhouse structures in the garden, where it was a great pleasure to sit down in the shade, surrounded by wonderful scents and a wilderness of blossom. The birds and the butterflies loved this place. It was no wonder the Langdons took such pride in the magnificent gardens they had achieved over generations in the wild, he thought. He had already quizzed Ava about many of the native plants, thinking they could do very well in the gardens of Villaflores.

"Well?" He gave her a soft, tender look, fighting down his inner rage at the damage Selwyn had done.

Ava bit her lip. "I don't really know where to begin."

"'Begin at the beginning and go on till you come to the end: then stop,'" he said humorously, quoting Lewis Carroll.

She had to smile. "You're always surprising me, Varo."

"I've got another one of Carroll's," he said, much more seriously. "'I can't go back to yesterday, because I was a different person then.'"

Tears came to her eyes as though they were saying goodbye. "That's true, isn't it?" she said. "But no matter what you do—what you decide to do—no matter where you go, I will never forget you, Varo."

He frowned, then said, "So what is this? You're telling me to go?" She had that look about her. She was so pale. Was she about to break his heart?

"No, no," Ava cried out in a kind of agony. "I thought you would *want* to go. I thought you might have some lingering doubts. Luke is such an accomplished liar. He's made lying an art form."

"You think I doubt you?" Varo asked in amazement. "I may have briefly considered you had a miscarriage and couldn't bear to talk about it. I would understand that. But the rest—never! You are my dearest, most beloved Ava. I trust you with my life. I trust you with my heart. Here—I give it to you." He cupped his elegant hands, held them out to her. His accent was becoming more and more pronounced as his feelings grew. "You *cannot* turn me away. I won't allow it." There was real worry on his stunning face.

"Let you go? You're crazy!" Ava exclaimed, letting her head fall against his shoulder. "I love you, Varo. You are the most wonderful thing that has happened to me in all my life. I would never have experienced *love*—true, undying love—if I hadn't met you. You *can't* go away." She gripped him around the waist, tried to shake him. "I won't let you. The first pregnancy I will ever have—the first baby I will ever hold—will be part of *you*. *Our* child. I should tell you I want at least four children. Two boys, Two girls. I think that should do it."

Varo stared into her lovely face, his expression deeply serious. He chose that very moment to slip out of her arms, only to drop onto one knee before her. "Some of us are greatly blessed in life," he said with emotion, because he was not a man who was afraid of emotion. "We find our soul mate. You are mine, Ava. I beg you to do me the honour of becoming my wife. Moreover, I insist on it. We will be married wherever you like. If you can't leave your homeland, I will—"

Ava leaned forward and sealed her mouth to his. It was a deep kiss, with an intensity of which there was no doubt. After a while she lifted her shining blonde head, her whole being aglow. "'For whither thou goest, I will go; and where thou lodgest, I will lodge: thy people shall be my people, and thy God, my God,'" she quoted. "I certainly believe in Him. He brought me *you*."

She held out her hands in a gesture of raising Varo to his feet. Then she too stood, to go into his waiting arms. They closed strongly, protectively, adoringly around her.

The moving finger had written. Time now for it to move on.

This was their destiny. They were ready to accept it and all life's challenges head-on. The power of love was awesome. It would overcome all else.

EPILOGUE

WHEN Karen Devereaux was asked by Luke Selwyn to back his shocking claim she refused point-blank, livid with outrage. None of it could be proved. She just *knew* Luke Selwyn had made it all up. Ava had never breathed a word to her about any pregnancy because she had never fallen pregnant to Luke. Karen was furious, deeply resenting the fact Luke was trying to use her. It would be much better if she broke off their so-called friendship.

Word was Ava and Varo were having two wedding ceremonies: one at Kooraki, the other at the Estancia de Villaflores in Argentina. She dearly wanted to go to both. There was even a chance Ava might ask her to be one of the bridesmaids. She had seen a great deal of Europe, the United States and Canada, but she had never been to South America. This was a wonderful opportunity to go.

Dev and Amelia were back from their honeymoon. There was bound to be a *huge* engagement party. She and Ava had always been close. Now she would make it her business to draw closer to Amelia, the mistress of Kooraki. Hadn't they always been a trio? Really good friends? She had always loved and cared for her cousin Ava. Or so she told herself. Luke Selwyn was someone from the past…

* * * * *

Mills & Boon® Hardback

July 2012

ROMANCE

The Secrets She Carried	Lynne Graham
To Love, Honour and Betray	Jennie Lucas
Heart of a Desert Warrior	Lucy Monroe
Unnoticed and Untouched	Lynn Raye Harris
A Royal World Apart	Maisey Yates
Distracted by her Virtue	Maggie Cox
The Count's Prize	Christina Hollis
The Tarnished Jewel of Jazaar	Susanna Carr
Keeping Her Up All Night	Anna Cleary
The Rules of Engagement	Ally Blake
Argentinian in the Outback	Margaret Way
The Sheriff's Doorstep Baby	Teresa Carpenter
The Sheikh's Jewel	Melissa James
The Rebel Rancher	Donna Alward
Always the Best Man	Fiona Harper
How the Playboy Got Serious	Shirley Jump
Sydney Harbour Hospital: Marco's Temptation	Fiona McArthur
Dr Tall, Dark...and Dangerous?	Lynne Marshall

MEDICAL

The Legendary Playboy Surgeon	Alison Roberts
Falling for Her Impossible Boss	Alison Roberts
Letting Go With Dr Rodriguez	Fiona Lowe
Waking Up With His Runaway Bride	Louisa George

Mills & Boon® Large Print

July 2012

ROMANCE

Roccanti's Marriage Revenge	Lynne Graham
The Devil and Miss Jones	Kate Walker
Sheikh Without a Heart	Sandra Marton
Savas's Wildcat	Anne McAllister
A Bride for the Island Prince	Rebecca Winters
The Nanny and the Boss's Twins	Barbara McMahon
Once a Cowboy...	Patricia Thayer
When Chocolate Is Not Enough...	Nina Harrington

HISTORICAL

The Mysterious Lord Marlowe	Anne Herries
Marrying the Royal Marine	Carla Kelly
A Most Unladylike Adventure	Elizabeth Beacon
Seduced by Her Highland Warrior	Michelle Willingham

MEDICAL

The Boss She Can't Resist	Lucy Clark
Heart Surgeon, Hero...Husband?	Susan Carlisle
Dr Langley: Protector or Playboy?	Joanna Neil
Daredevil and Dr Kate	Leah Martyn
Spring Proposal in Swallowbrook	Abigail Gordon
Doctor's Guide to Dating in the Jungle	Tina Beckett

Mills & Boon® Hardback
August 2012

ROMANCE

Contract with Consequences	Miranda Lee
The Sheikh's Last Gamble	Trish Morey
The Man She Shouldn't Crave	Lucy Ellis
The Girl He'd Overlooked	Cathy Williams
A Tainted Beauty	Sharon Kendrick
One Night With The Enemy	Abby Green
The Dangerous Jacob Wilde	Sandra Marton
His Last Chance at Redemption	Michelle Conder
The Hidden Heart of Rico Rossi	Kate Hardy
Marrying the Enemy	Nicola Marsh
Mr Right, Next Door!	Barbara Wallace
The Cowboy Comes Home	Patricia Thayer
The Rancher's Housekeeper	Rebecca Winters
Her Outback Rescuer	Marion Lennox
Monsoon Wedding Fever	Shoma Narayanan
If the Ring Fits...	Jackie Braun
Sydney Harbour Hospital: Ava's Re-Awakening	Carol Marinelli
How To Mend A Broken Heart	Amy Andrews

MEDICAL

Falling for Dr Fearless	Lucy Clark
The Nurse He Shouldn't Notice	Susan Carlisle
Every Boy's Dream Dad	Sue MacKay
Return of the Rebel Surgeon	Connie Cox

Mills & Boon® Large Print

August 2012

ROMANCE

A Deal at the Altar	Lynne Graham
Return of the Moralis Wife	Jacqueline Baird
Gianni's Pride	Kim Lawrence
Undone by His Touch	Annie West
The Cattle King's Bride	Margaret Way
New York's Finest Rebel	Trish Wylie
The Man Who Saw Her Beauty	Michelle Douglas
The Last Real Cowboy	Donna Alward
The Legend of de Marco	Abby Green
Stepping out of the Shadows	Robyn Donald
Deserving of His Diamonds?	Melanie Milburne

HISTORICAL

The Scandalous Lord Lanchester	Anne Herries
Highland Rogue, London Miss	Margaret Moore
His Compromised Countess	Deborah Hale
The Dragon and the Pearl	Jeannie Lin
Destitute On His Doorstep	Helen Dickson

MEDICAL

Sydney Harbour Hospital: Lily's Scandal	Marion Lennox
Sydney Harbour Hospital: Zoe's Baby	Alison Roberts
Gina's Little Secret	Jennifer Taylor
Taming the Lone Doc's Heart	Lucy Clark
The Runaway Nurse	Dianne Drake
The Baby Who Saved Dr Cynical	Connie Cox